Twin Souls

-Book One of the Nevermore Series-

By K.A. Poe

An Original Publication Of FROSTBITE PUBLISHING

 A Frostbite book published by
FROSTEBITE PUBLISHING
PO Box 4435, Arizona City, AZ 85123

ISBN-13: 978-1500472948
ISBN-10: 1500472948

Second U.S. Paperback Edition, 2014

Printed in the United States of America

Visit www.frostbitepublishing.com

For business inquiries, please contact Frostbite Publishing at
fbp@frostbitepublishing.com

To my dearest Adam – without your encouragement and assistance, this dream may never have become a reality.

All my love ~

Twin Souls

-Book One of the Nevermore Series-

By K.A. Poe

The Letter

The rough pitter-patter of rain against the tin roof caused me to stir in my sleep, but I struggled to fight it. I yearned to remain under the warmth of my thick quilt, wandering aimlessly through the dream world. But, alas, I knew reality would ease its way in and pull me out. As hard as I tried to ignore it, my eyes flew open and all memory of dreams faded away. I sighed heavily and pressed my pillow hard against my eyes, blocking out the dim sunlight that snuck in through the creases in the blinds. Slowly, I pushed away my brief shelter from the light and let my eyes adjust. I stumbled to the bathroom, rinsed my face and brushed my teeth before swiftly walking downstairs to the kitchen.

I was surprised to find it empty, void of any evidence that my mother had even been there fifteen minutes prior. Most mornings I would find her sitting at the quaint glass table, pressed up against the far wall, sipping a quick cup of coffee before she rushed off to work. My mother didn't hold the greatest job title in the world, but the money was sufficient enough to pay the bills and to feed us. She worked as a zookeeper at the local zoo and had been in that same position for as far back as I could remember. My father isn't even worth mentioning. After I turned six, he became absent in my life, beyond the occasional postcard from wherever he happened to be at the time. During a mid-life crisis, he decided that "living his life to the fullest" was more important than his ten-year marriage, not to mention his six-year-old daughter. Now he spent his time traveling the world with his much younger and wealthy girlfriend, Melissa. I hated to even think of her, though I had never even met her.

As I thought over my mother's unexpected absence, I plucked a porcelain blue bowl from the cupboard and poured a generous amount of cereal and milk into it before sitting at the vacant table. My eyes were instantly drawn to the white, perfectly folded note that lay against the transparent surface. Sprawled across the paper in my mom's unmistakable handwriting was my name: Alexis.

I wasn't sure why, but something, deep down, told me that this couldn't be good. Something was wrong, and this letter was the only way I would find out just what it was. I swallowed hard as I lifted the crisp paper and unfolded it. Panic welled up inside as I read the first sentence.

'Dear Alexis, September 8, 2012
This isn't easy for me to say, and it won't be easy for you to hear either.'

Part of me didn't want to continue reading, but my eyes betrayed me as they went along down the paper.

'The house has been put in your name, and I have left an envelope on the counter beside the coffee pot where you will find enough money to support yourself for at least the next three months. I will send you more as needed. Do you

remember Mark? The man who offered me the job in Denver? I know how hard it was on you when you heard that we might have to move, and I decided that this might be easier. I will be making twice as much there as I was here, and won't have any trouble paying for you to stay home. Mark and I are moving in together.'

My forehead creased as the last words sunk in. Mom had a boyfriend, and I didn't even know about it ...

'You are not alone, Alexis. You have your friends, and your uncle Paul is still in town if you need someone. I didn't want you to sacrifice your school life and your friends just so that I could live a better life, with a better job, and a better man than your father ever was. I won't be that far away if you ever need me.
    Forgive me.
    Love,
    Mom'

My head was spinning as I set the letter down. I accidentally knocked over my cereal bowl as I scrambled to run back upstairs. It didn't matter anymore – my appetite had vanished. I pushed open my mother's bedroom door, and my jaw dropped in shock. While her bed remained intact, covered with frilly pillows and bright-colored blankets, her dresser was empty of most of her belongings. The oak jewelry box that held all the beautiful necklaces and charms I had been so envious of was no longer there. I went through her drawers. Each one was empty. How had she left so quietly, without me knowing?
    I sat on the edge of her plush mattress, my head in my hands as I tried to understand what was happening. Mom

and I were never incredibly close as she spent so much time at work – and I guess hanging out with Mark – but I would have thought she would have had the decency to sit down with me and discuss the situation before abandoning me. Abandoning me ... just like dad.

Through the creases of my fingers, I could see the red digits on one of the few remaining items in her room. On top of the dresser sat her alarm clock, and I could distinctly see the shapes of each number: 9:45. I immediately jumped up from the bed and ran to my room. I was late for school! I grabbed my book bag, pulled on my shoes, snatched my car keys from the kitchen counter and rushed through the front door.

I grimaced when I noticed the windows on my silver Alero were rolled down, and the rain had undoubtedly found its way into the car. Remorsefully, I eyed the empty spot where my mother's van would have been parked, then opened the driver-side door to my car. I was hopeful that school would be a big enough distraction to keep my mind off of the haunting thought of being abandoned by my mother. The overwhelming urge to stay home, retreat back to my bed, and spend the day crying the hours away was almost too tempting. School wasn't a great importance to me, but I hoped that seeing my friends might help me pull through.

Shaking away the unwelcome thoughts, I discovered that my suspicions were unfortunately right—the seats were drenched. After pulling off my gray fleece hoodie, I dabbed the moisture off of the steering wheel then draped the clothing across the seat. Once situated, I closed the door and quickly rolled up the windows and started the ignition. Some classical music piece came streaming through the speakers, and I smiled. I found it relaxing, but I wouldn't admit that to any of my friends at school.

Music Class

Driving to school didn't take long – it never did – where I lived was, for the most part, a tiny speck of a town. My family had resided in Willowshire, Colorado for many generations. According to my mother, this had been where my great-great-great grandparents grew up. It had once been nothing but forest, mountain and rivers until a small group of people began using the area for cattle farms. From there, the little valley nestled between Silverton and Telluride slowly developed into what it is today. Although small in comparison to most towns, we have our own small shopping center with an old movie theatre, a grocery store, and of course—schools. In the last couple of years the town has started to develop more and more, and yet somehow it manages to hold onto a lot of what makes the town beautiful. The snow-capped mountains in the distance tower over the town, and much of the forestry continues to exist throughout. Willowshire holds a small population of maybe 3,000 people, and it is uncommon to meet someone you don't recognize.

As I turned into the school parking lot, I switched the music station to something more recent. Whatever the song was; I didn't like it. Being late, the high school parking lot was full, and I had to park away from the building. In my rush, I had forgotten to bring an umbrella, so I carried my book bag over my head as I sloshed through the puddles on my way to the school doors. Fortunately, the water wasn't deep enough to soak through my shoes. I rushed through the front doors; my sneakers skidding slightly on the linoleum floors. The front hall was empty, aside from the janitor – Mr. Leary – who was mopping up puddles and muddied spots. I apologized earnestly for making more of a mess as I ran to my English class.

The teacher scolded me for being late, shaking her head as her gaze followed me to my seat. Her name was Mrs. Donovan, and she was by far my least favorite teacher, which was unfortunate because it was my favorite subject. She was a middle-aged woman with spectacles that reminded me of those you would see on a little old lady.

It took me a few minutes to realize what the assignment was, but once Mrs. Donovan said the name 'Poe', I was instantly on board. It was the first-time Edgar Allan Poe's works were brought up in this class, and I was a big fan so this caught my attention. We were supposed to be reading *The Raven,* and I realized I didn't have a book with me.

I raised my hand sheepishly.

"Yes, Miss Hobbs?" the teacher said coldly.

"I don't have a book," I replied, and noticed everyone had turned to stare at me. My cheeks instantly grew red.

"You can read from my copy," she waltzed over to my desk and flopped the worn book onto the wooden surface.

"Thanks," I said meekly and began flipping through the volume until I found the right page. I had become engulfed in the story, unaware of how quickly time was passing. I jumped when the bell rang and reluctantly put the book down.

"We will continue reading next week, Miss Hobbs," Mrs. Donovan said as she pried the book from my hand.

"Right," I mumbled and noticed that the classroom was deserted aside from us. I rushed out of the room and headed toward biology. I barely paid any attention to what was happening as the teacher droned on about heart vessels and other things I didn't care about. Next was lunch, and I was beyond excited to get out of the classroom.

The cafeteria was packed full of students. After gathering my tray of food, I walked slowly toward my usual table. Sitting there were my two closest friends, Jason and Karen.

Karen was your typical teenage girl – she loved to shop, to flirt, and to gossip. Somehow, however, we got along. We had known each other since we were toddlers, and lived as neighbors for nearly ten years before my mom decided to relocate to my current house. She was tall, stick-thin, with green eyes and perfectly straight, long blonde hair that she always wore in braids or a ponytail.

Jason, on the other hand, was somewhat different from the typical high school boy. He was smart, but I wouldn't classify him as a geek. He enjoyed sports, but I wouldn't consider him a jock, either. He had a love for literature, art, and most of all – partying. Jason was almost a jumble of every high school stereotype put into one body. We had been friends for nearly as long as Karen and I had. We met in kindergarten, and the three of us became inseparable. While some girls considered him highly attractive, he was just another guy to me, possibly because of our close friendship. He was slightly shorter than Karen (which I often teased him for), with a slight muscular build. Every member of his family had the same dark brunette hair with the faintest hint of a golden highlight; his hair was chin-length and wavy towards the ends. His eyes were a shade of brown that reminded me of milk chocolate.

"Hey, Alex," Jason said with a grin, until he noticed my disappointed expression. "What's wrong?"

"It's nothing," I said quietly, but knew he would pry it out of me one way or another.

"I'm not letting you off that easy," he objected.

"Fine," I eyed the food on my tray before pushing it away, "mom left." I tried to stop myself from falling apart as I spoke the words out loud for the first time.

"What?" Karen piped in, having previously been distracted by one of the boys across the room, which was typical for her.

"She took the job in Denver that I was telling you about last week," I studied their faces, "don't worry. I'm not going anywhere."

"Where are you going to live?" Karen frowned, wrapping her arms around me in a sympathetic hug. "You can come stay with me if you need to. My parents have always said that you could stay whenever you wanted."

"No, it's okay," I said, my disappointed look evolving into a half-hearted smile. "She gave me the house ... "

"You have your own house?" Jason gaped.

"I guess so," I grinned. "She's paying for it, too."

"Wow ... " Karen whispered.

"So, when is the first party?" Jason smirked.

"I don't think I'll be throwing any parties any time soon, Jason."

"C'mon ... I'll do all the work!" he pleaded. "I'll make the invitations, get the food ... you just have to provide the place!"

I laughed. "I'll think about it."

My appetite finally came back, and I was able to down a pudding cup before the bell rang again.

"I'll see you two in the gym." I waved as I walked off to music class.

My friends knew I was in music class, but as far as they were aware I hated it. Music was my passion, but I had my doubts that anything would ever come from it in terms of a career. Simply listening to a piece of classical music, or inventing my own, was enough to make me happy. Unfortunately, my mother could never afford to buy me a piano of my own, so most of my practice was done at school. There was also a period of my life where I took piano lessons, but after my father left I lost interest in it as well as many other hobbies. After a few years, I came to realize that Desmond wasn't returning, and I had to carry on with my life and rediscovered my joy of playing. I don't know why I felt so compelled to keep my love of classical music a secret. Maybe I was worried my friends would tease me for it, as they had done with other kids. I walked briskly into the class, excited to practice on the piano again. I had been improving greatly, and I was looking forward to getting my fingers on the keys.

To my despair, we had a substitute teacher who didn't appear to have a clue what he was doing.

"Mr. Collins won't be in today," the teacher announced when the class was seated. He had a bulging round belly, and pants held up by suspenders. His head was round, with a very evident receding hairline. "My name is Mr. Knotts, and I will be filling in as best as I can, but I must apologize ahead of time – I am usually the astronomy teacher and have never touched an instrument in my life."

"Then what do you expect us to do today?" The words came out of my mouth before I had the chance to stop myself. This wasn't uncommon for me, and I had been scolded on the habit far too many times – enough that I should have learned by now to keep my mouth shut.

"I-well ... " the sub stuttered, ignoring my rudeness, and his puffy cheeks reddened. "I suppose you can just play whatever music you want until the bell rings," he replied with a shrug of his thick shoulders.

The class laughed; myself included. I shrugged and walked over to one of the pianos – there were two of them in the classroom, as well as a keyboard. The one I selected had obvious wear to it, no doubt donated to the school by an employee or some sort of foundation. This was usually the one I chose to play on; something about it lured me to it the very day I began this class. I placed my hands on the keys, feeling comfortable and at ease as I gently ran my fingers along them. I played an unfamiliar tune, something that simply came to me as my fingers did their magic. I noticed that everyone had their eyes in my direction, and I stopped abruptly.

"That is magnificent," someone said beside me. I could distinctly hear what I thought must have been a British accent mingled in their voice, "If not a tad melancholic," they added.

"Um, thank you." I blushed.

"Whose was it?"

"Mine," I said quietly, almost wishing I had stuck to something well known to avoid the attention. Then I looked up, astonished by what I saw. Sitting next to me on the bench was a student I had never seen before in this class ... or in the entire school, for that matter. He had a pleasant smile that ceased to fade as he stared at me through light blue eyes. He came into full focus – short, shaggy black hair that fell across his pale face, a long-sleeved burgundy V-neck shirt that hung loosely against his thin body, black slacks and a brilliant smile. His appearance was very unfitting for this school ... maybe he was dressed for a meeting at the drama club after school or something.

"Where did you learn to play so well?" he asked, and I noticed how silky his voice was.

"My mom put me through lessons when I was a kid. The rest I learned here," I answered confidently.

"I am impressed."

"I've never seen you here before," I spat out, without meaning to. I looked away suddenly.

"That is because I have never been here until today," he replied and unexpectedly put his hand to my chin and turned my face back toward him. "I find you very intriguing."

I blinked. "What?"

"I will see you later."

"No, wait!" However, it was too late; he was already exiting the room as the words escaped my mouth.

As I pondered this unfamiliar new student, I continued playing on the piano – this time choosing something less conspicuous, and before I knew it, the bell was ringing. Stopping playing, I couldn't help but notice some students were staring in my direction still and talking in hushed voices. Clearly, it hadn't solely been my music that had caught their attention, but the out-of-place new kid as well. I sat there a few moments longer, still somewhat in shock from the encounter with this new boy, as I watched the rest of the students flood through the classroom door. After I gathered my thoughts, I exited the room and raced toward the gym.

Salem

I met Jason and Karen on the bleachers, where I tied my shoelaces that had somewhere along the way come undone. Karen stared at me inquisitively.

"What's up, Alex?" she asked as I hopped off of the bleachers.

"Not much," I answered. "Just wondering who this new kid is that I met in music class."

"Some music nerd, huh?" Jason snickered.

My eyes lowered to the ground when he said that, but I tried to ignore the comment. "No. He was ... different," I said difficultly, trying not to show my true emotions toward what he had said.

"Different how?" Karen asked as she passed me a volleyball. I sighed, hating sports with a passion.

I hit the ball over the net absentmindedly as I talked to my friends. "There was just something strange about him ... I don't know."

"I haven't noticed any new kids in any of my classes," Jason said as he deflected the incoming ball, sending it back over the net with ease.

"Me either," Karen agreed.

"Maybe he isn't in any of your classes," I said, but I knew that was near impossible. The school wasn't that big. Willowshire High School held a student body count of maybe a hundred kids.

As the volleyball game was coming to an end, Jason and Karen pulled me along to the bleachers again. We each sat there, catching our breath when the inevitable happened – Jason brought up the subject I knew was coming.

"So, when's the party?" he grinned.

"There isn't going to be a party, Jace."

"It won't be a problem at all; I swear!" he practically begged.

"Fine. Sunday night." I gave in with a worried frown. "That gives you two days to plan, so you better hurry. And no alcohol!"

"Yes, ma'am!" he said triumphantly, "I'll catch up with you two later. I have to head home, lots of planning to do!"

"See you later," Karen and I said in unison.

"Do you want me to ride home with you?" she asked as we watched Jason exit the gymnasium.

"Why would I want that?"

"I just thought." She paused momentarily, and then continued, "That since your mom is gone ... you might get lonely," she said sorrowfully.

I smiled up at her, but shook my head. "It's all right. A night alone might do me some good. Maybe I'll call her and straighten things out ... "

"All right. I'll see you next week, then." She gave me a quick worried glance, a quick hug, and then turned and left.

And there I was, alone on the bleachers. I reluctantly got up and walked off to my locker to collect my book bag. As I slowly walked through the gym, I considered the possibility of calling my mom when I returned home. What would I even say to her, though? I was certain I wouldn't be able to control my fury and hurt, that it would begin with an outburst of accusations on how she decided her plans were more important, how Mark was more significant than me ... and then it dawned on me how similar this felt to when dad abandoned us eleven years ago. Had she realized this? I could feel the warmth of tears welling up behind my eyes, and it was hard to hold it back as the pain and knowing seeped in. Was I doing something wrong to cause my parents to leave me? My pace quickened as I felt the tears trickling down my cheeks. I had to get out of here, before someone noticed ...

The sun had decided to peek out through the clouds a little, and I was pleased to see the puddles were starting to dry up. The water on the asphalt was deeper than this morning; however, and I could feel the moisture seeping into my shoes. I was about four feet from my car before my feet were completely soaked. The tears were drying against my skin, and I hoped no one would notice as I passed through the parking lot. I stopped abruptly when I saw the boy from music class leaning up against the Alero. I gulped and cautiously walked up to him.

"What are you doing?" I asked suspiciously.

"I was waiting for you," he said simply. As I looked him over, I noticed his clothing wasn't damp and his feet were not soaked, unlike mine. How had he managed to get through the parking lot unscathed?

My brows furrowed. "And how'd you know this was my car?"

"One of your friends told me."

"Oh, really?" I asked, "Which one?"

He paused to think, as if he couldn't quite place the name. "A tall, blonde-haired girl."

"Karen ... " I whispered.

"Ah, yes. That was it." He beamed. "She also mentioned that tomorrow is a special day for you."

"I told her not to tell anyone ... "

"Why would you do that?" He seemed genuinely confused.

"I've just never really liked birthdays is all," I muttered, eying him curiously. "And why in the world would she tell *you* of all people that anyway?"

"But you are blessed with another year of life." He smiled brilliantly at me and ignored my question, then unexpectedly said, "I want to take you somewhere, if you are willing. On the other hand, perhaps I should say I would like for you to take me somewhere, I suppose."

"I don't even know you, and you want me to take you somewhere?" I was bewildered and yet enthralled that this boy was even talking to me.

"We can introduce each other on the way," he offered.

I shook my head, uncertain. "Maybe some other time."

"It has to be now," he insisted.

"Give me one good reason why it has to be now."

"There's no time like the present?" he suggested with a grin. "Tomorrow you could be gone, or I could be gone, and then we would never have this opportunity again."

"Sure," I said as I took in his words. A sudden feeling of needing to do as he asked washed over me. "But I'm driving," I added.

The boy eyed the car and nodded. "It is probably best that way, and as I corrected myself – I want you to take me somewhere."

"You don't know how to drive?" I inquired as I unlocked the passenger-side door for him.

"That's one way to put it." He smiled lightly as he sat down.

I walked over to the driver side and climbed in, started the ignition and glanced over at him. There was something comforting about his presence, but I couldn't quite place what it was. He directed me toward wherever our destination was, which eventually led us down a winding road that made me very nervous to drive on. We passed a field of feasting cows near a small, broken-down house, and then everything grew into dense forest and rock.

"Where are we going?"

"You will see. It is just a little further," he said, gazing out the window at the scenery, although he must have seen it lots of times before, or so I assumed.

I thought for a moment about just turning around. Had I been tricked by some serial killer or rapist in my moment of vulnerability from this morning's events? I glanced over at the stranger in my car for a brief moment; he seemed harmless enough, sitting there with his ever-present smile. The thoughts of uncertainty fell loose from my mind and I focused back on the road and listened to the directions I was being given.

I became increasingly anxious as we rode down the twisting, thin road. The asphalt suddenly evolved into a dirt road that felt like it went on for miles and miles ahead of us. I hadn't noticed the turn to our left until he pointed it out. I slowly jerked the car down the new path, and we were soon approaching a tall, beautiful Victorian house planted in the middle of the blossoming foliage.

"Where are we?" I asked in an awed voice.

"My home," he said pleasantly. "But before we enter, I made you a promise. My name is Salem Young," he explained bitterly, which by the look on his face, I assumed he hoped I hadn't noticed.

"You don't like your name?" I asked.

"I suppose that is what you would say," he answered. "It is somewhat contradictory."

"Contradictory to what?" I asked, confused.

"You will find out soon enough," he said. "Your name is Alexis Hobbs."

"I take it Karen told you that, too, did she?" I asked with a grimace.

He ignored my question, climbed out of the car and quickly walked to my side, opened the door and offered me his hand.

I thought for a moment before I reluctantly took his hand, barely noticing the difference in his skin's temperature. He smiled as he gracefully led me to the alabaster stairs. We climbed up the stairway, and I stared, mystified, at the tall white doors. The windows were stained glass images of what I recognized to be Celtic knots in beautiful shades of blues and greens. Salem grasped the brass door handle and swiftly opened the large doors, revealing an immaculate living area. The walls were painted a dull gray that perfectly contrasted the white sectional sofa pushed up against the furthest wall. Behind the couch was a wide window overlooking a lake. In front of the couch lay a large black rug that covered the otherwise white tiled floor, and atop the rug was a rectangular glass coffee table. I was somewhat surprised not to see a TV anywhere.

On the other side of the room was a vast bookshelf, every inch of which was crammed with books of all sizes. An armchair identical in color to the sectional sofa sat nestled in a small nook beside the bookcase. Beside the chair was a tall, silver floor lamp. As I was admiring the room, Salem came up behind me and grasped my shoulders. I jumped, startled by his touch, but relaxed as he spun me around toward a spiral staircase that led upstairs. It wasn't the staircase that caught my attention, but the large, white grand piano that sat to the right of it.

"It's beautiful ... " I said in a mere whisper. "Is your family rich or something?

"What?" He looked shocked at my assumption, but his expression turned soft, and he smiled as he seemed to do more often than not. "I don't live with my family."

"Then *you* are rich?" I questioned, staring at him in awe.

"Not at all."

"Then how do you afford to live here?"

"You'll find out soon enough," he repeated and turned toward the kitchen, waving me to follow.

Mahogany cabinets lined the back walls, and a black refrigerator and stove stood out amongst them. A small dining table was set against a broad window. The curtains were drawn, but the room was still bright despite there being no lights on.

After I allowed myself to admire the house, I realized how soaked my feet still were. "Do you care if I take these off?" I asked shyly.

"Of course not."

I walked to the front door, cringing with each step as the water sloshed around in my shoes. I opened the doors, knelt down and untied the moist laces. I looked up and contemplated just running to my car and leaving this place behind for good. If this boy, no doubt the same age as myself, was staying in a place like this with no family and no money

• • •

of his own, then maybe my once seemingly crazy suspicions were right. For all I knew he had found this place and killed the previous inhabitants, and I had just been unlucky enough to be the next random victim he had chosen.

Before I had time to think about fleeing anymore, the door behind me cracked open slightly and his smooth voice came gliding out. "Is everything okay?"

"Yeah, I … these shoes are just kind of stuck," I lied as I tugged them off, pretending it was harder than it really was. It was too late to run to the car now, and the calming sensation flushed trough me again—I felt again as if I truly wanted to be here.

After removing my wet socks and hanging them over the banister, I followed Salem back inside and into the immense kitchen where he abruptly spun around to face me. "Tomorrow, everything will change," he said suddenly. I gulped, not liking the serious tone in his voice. I should have run when I had the chance.

"I'll just be turning eighteen," I said as I stepped back slightly.

"You will be a whole different person." His eyes were withdrawn now, and the once permanent smile had faded. "And I will be partially at fault."

"What are you talking about Salem?" I could hear the panic in my voice as I tried to step back once again but was unable to move.

"Don't worry, Alexis." He smiled somberly. "Once the clock strikes midnight, I can tell you everything."

"Midnight?!" I almost laughed, despite my nerves. "You expect me to stay here until *midnight?!*"

"Only if you will."

"Why midnight?"

"Don't make me say it again." He smirked. I could distinctly hear his voice in my head repeating '*You'll find out soon enough*'.

I looked at the simple black-banded watch on my right wrist. It was only now seven o'clock. It wasn't so much that I needed to get back home, but how could I possibly stay here with this stranger for the next five hours? I glanced up into his eyes, and I saw something alluring and comforting ... the need to stay was becoming overwhelmingly strong. Even so, when I let myself think it through, I knew this had to be a mistake, and I couldn't help continuously coming back to the possibility that this boy was far more lethal than he looked. Something blocked those thoughts.

"Do you have someplace to be?" he asked, before I had the chance to speak.

"No ... " It came out in barely a whisper as it had finally sunk in that I had no one to go to anymore. Mom was gone; home would be vacant and lonely. I should have agreed to have Karen ride home with me after all. I fought back the moisture in my eyes, biting down on my lip and trying to force myself to suppress my feelings again.

"At least stay long enough to play that tune for me again," he said, almost pleadingly.

Coincidences

Hesitantly, I agreed to stay and play my song for Salem. He sat beside me on the wooden bench as I placed my hands on the keys. I shut my eyes as I played flawlessly – even to my own amazement, considering I had only come up with it this afternoon in school. I stopped abruptly when I felt his hands reaching across and touching mine. With a sudden gasp, my eyes flew open—his fingers were freezing! He smiled warmly at me, and I forgot all about the cold to his touch and returned to playing, his hands following the movement of my own. I relaxed a little as I continued to play, until at last the song was through; he didn't remove his hands.

"I still cannot get over how beautiful it is," he said quietly as he peered into my eyes.

"Um ... th-thank you," I whispered, my cheeks growing warm. I glanced at my watch: 7:15. I sighed.

"What's wrong?" Salem asked, and then noticed where my eyes were looking. "Oh. Anxious for it to be midnight?"

"I guess so, yeah," I said with uncertainty.

He nodded and slid off of the bench. "Are you hungry?"

"A little," I replied honestly, before I had the chance to think better of it. There was a nagging in the back of my mind, a faint worry that he might have intentions of poisoning me.

"If you could have anything right now, what would it be?"

I laughed as I thought about it. "Umm ... chocolate cheesecake drizzled with caramel."

Salem shrugged. "I will see what I have." Before he turned toward the kitchen, I could have sworn I saw a glint of violet in his eyes, but I ignored it—it was probably my imagination playing tricks on me. He walked into the kitchen, tugging me gently behind him. As he opened the black door of the fridge, my hand dropped from his grasp, and I stood frozen in shock. Sitting on a glass plate on the top shelf of the fridge was a slice of delectable cheesecake, just as I had described it. I shook my head in disbelief. I barely noticed that the rest of the fridge was empty.

"How?" My voice barely came out.

"Coincident?" he smiled. "Go ahead, eat it."

"How do I know you didn't poison it?" I gasped, letting my prior thoughts free.

The look of hurt in his eyes made me regret it instantly. "You think I would poison you?" he frowned. "Would you like me to eat some of it to prove it is harmless?"

I nodded my head slowly, still unable to completely convince myself this strange boy had my best interest in mind, regardless of how kindly he had treated me so far—it could have all been a trap.

Salem shook his head in disappointment, but I watched him pull open a drawer. Wielding a silver fork, he gathered some of the cake and put it to his lips. I watched, my heart pounding, as he chewed the luscious chocolate, and he smiled up at me. "See? It is perfectly safe."

"Okay." I gave in and took a bite. It was even better than I had imagined. I tried to fight the urge to eat the entire slice, but it was impossible. It was quite possibly the greatest food I had ever tasted. "Are you a chef?"

He laughed; the sound was musical, beautiful ... I wanted to hear it again. "No, but I will have to let the Baker at Budwell's Bakery know you appreciate his work."

"I still don't understand how you had a piece of cake just like the one I wanted just lying around in the fridge," I said, wiping my mouth of chocolaty residue.

He shrugged. "I told you ... purely coincidental."

"Right ... " I said as we walked into the wide, open living room. He laid out on the end of the sectional, and I sat on the opposite side. Part of me wouldn't have minded being closer to him, but I felt distance was safest at this point. I contemplated what could possibly happen at midnight, how it would change anything, and how this boy could be involved in any way.

"How long have you lived here, Salem?" I asked out of the blue.

"A few years," he replied, putting his hands behind his head. He looked comfortable, serene. Strands of black hair fell across his eyes, shrouding them from my view.

"Did you just start going to our school today or something?"

He didn't respond right away. "No," he answered simply.

"Were you going to a different one before?"

"Yes." Just as simply.

I glanced at my watch again: 8:13.

* * *

"Sooo … tell me about yourself," I said as I watched the second hand on my watch tick slowly by.

"I don't have much to tell you right now," he said in a strange voice, "that will have to wait until the right time."

"Midnight, right?" I laughed, but I wasn't really amused.

"Perhaps." He lifted his head to look at me, "I'm not sure what I can tell you, to be honest. It isn't entirely for me to decide."

"What are you even talking about?"

"It will be easier to explain come midnight," he assured me, but I was doubtful.

"Do you not own a TV?" I asked, growing bored.

"No. I have no use for one."

"What?" I laughed. "Everyone watches TV, or at least movies!"

"Do they?" he asked thoughtfully as he rested his head once more.

I sat and watched him lying there perfectly still, as time slowly crept by. I was tired – no, exhausted – and longed to return to that familiar place I reluctantly left this morning. This day had twisted in such a way that I never could have imagined. Mom was gone; I still couldn't grasp that fact. I had a house in my name. Jason wanted to throw a party, and I made the wretched mistake of agreeing! Then, I met this bizarre, yet fascinating boy … and ended up here. How did things turn out this way? I should have woken up in the morning, found mom at her usual spot at the table, left for school, had an ordinary day, gone home, watched TV and gone to bed.

"So," I said, interrupting the silence again, "seeing as you don't spend your free time watching TV like a normal person, what do you do?"

"I do plenty of things. A lot of my time is spent reading, hiking, listening to music, pondering our existence ... "

"You do have a pretty big collection of books, I see," I commented, eying the shelves of books. "What are your favorites?"

I could see a faint smile spread across his lips as he contemplated my question. "Hmm ... I suppose that might include some of Charles Dickens' literature, as well as Poe's masterpieces. *The Picture of Dorian Gray* and I must admit I have a soft spot for *Romeo and Juliet*."

With scarce realization, I felt myself smile. He shared interest in some of my favorite reads, but that shouldn't surprise me – considering he appeared to have tastes beyond his years, shown not only in his book collection but his choice of clothing and his love of the piano. "Those are some of my favorites, too," I replied, "Are you in the drama club at school or something?"

He glanced toward me and arched a brow, "While I enjoy the occasional play, I cannot picture myself upon a stage. Why do you ask?"

"You dress a lot differently than most kids our age."

"Our age," he mused, laughing to himself at some unspoken joke, "I suppose I just have a finer taste in clothing than the typical teenager."

"What about music? Do you play the piano?" I felt somewhat stupid asking, considering he did possess the very instrument.

"Occasionally, although I dare to say I am not nearly as exquisite a pianist as you are."

My cheeks reddened. "I'm not that good, really."

"I disagree. You have exceptional talent, Alexis." He smiled again. "You should put that to use, perhaps make a future out of it."

"Me? On stage?" I laughed at the thought. "There is no way I could get on stage in front of a crowd and play. I barely have the nerve to play at school in front of the music teacher. I just can't see myself doing that." I frowned.

"You never know, someday that might change."

"I wish I could look at it like that as easily as you can." I sighed. "Do you mind if I check out your bookshelf?"

"Be my guest."

I watched him closely as I rose from my seat. I walked across the plush rug and over to the bookshelf. To my relief, I found *The Raven* among the wide variety, but that didn't surprise me at all. I plopped myself down in the armchair, switched on the light and began to read from where I had left off at school. Before I knew it, I unintentionally dozed off.

Midnight

"Once upon a midnight dreary, while I pondered weak and weary, over many a quaint and curious volume of forgotten lore, while I nodded, nearly napping, suddenly there came a tapping, as of someone gently rapping, rapping at my chamber door." [- Edgar Allan Poe]

"Nevermore." I heard a silky voice whisper into my ear. A wisp of cool breath tickled against my neck, and I jumped. My eyes burned from exhaustion, and my heart was thumping hard in my chest.

"It wasn't all a dream, then," I said, somewhat disappointed but at the same time a little relieved.

Salem simply smiled at me. "It is midnight."

"It is?" I looked at my watch to be sure. "It is! I must have dozed off while reading. So ... what happens now?"

"Your mother didn't just leave on a whim," he said grimly, and quite suddenly.

I stared at him groggily. "What? You know my mom?"

"I met her once before," he said. "You might say I am familiar with her boyfriend more so than her. She left this letter with me, to give to you on your birthday."

"How did you know where to find me?"

"She told me where you would be, just read the letter."

I tore the letter open, my heart racing once more. How much agony was I going to have to endure before this was all over? I read down the letter, slowly taking in each word—

'Alexis, September 9th, 2012

Happy birthday, sweetie. I know the circumstances are a little different than you might have anticipated, but trust me – things are only going to get better. Paul was the one that insisted I leave – maybe not quite like this, but nevertheless, you shouldn't put the blame entirely on me. You can beat him up for that when you see him again.

I left a present for you with Salem, whom I hope has been kind enough to explain the situation with you more than this letter can. While having a house of your own with no expenses might seem like the perfect eighteenth birthday present, that was more of a gift to me than it was to you. I hope you like it and can find some use for it.

Visit Paul as soon as you can. You will understand even more clearly when you do.

Love always,
Mom'

Before I could ask, Salem passed me a present. This led me to believe he had read the letter, but I ignored that thought. I ripped the bright pink wrapping paper away, revealing a simple cardboard box. It wasn't taped, but the flaps had been folded so it wouldn't open. I popped up the flaps to reveal a black, leather-bound book. When I opened

TWIN SOULS

it, the pages were blank. I looked at Salem, as if he might have an answer for me.

"What is it?" he leaned over to have a peek.

"Is this some sort of diary?" I laughed. Mom should have known by now that I had no interest in a diary. I had never written in one before, why would I start now?

"I suppose it must be." he looked a little shocked, as if he was expecting something entirely different. "Whatever it is, your mom wanted you to have it and that's all that is important." He smiled.

"Please tell me this isn't what I waited all night for."

"It isn't." He glanced away from me; his eyes turned toward the vast window behind the sectional. "Now that you are eighteen, your mother thinks you can handle the truth." He sighed heavily. "I don't know why I was the one left with this task."

"The truth about what?" I demanded.

"Your heritage, your real family." He glanced up at me. "I know this is all very sudden, and it is going to be confusing and hurtful, but I need you to listen. Janet isn't your real mother, Alexis. Nor is Desmond your father."

I nearly laughed, but stopped myself when I noticed how serious Salem looked. "Of course they are my parents! I have been with them all my life!"

He smiled warmly and took my hand, leading me to the sofa. I sat down hesitantly beside him. "Paul is your real father."

"As in my *uncle* Paul?" I shook my head and laughed. "That's impossible. Is this some sort of prank or something?"

"Think about it, Alexis."

And I did. I thought hard, picturing Desmond and Janet in my mind. I looked nothing at all like them. My father was dark-skinned, lanky and there was no

• • •
38

resemblance between him and me. My mother and I may have shared the same dark brunette hair and light complexion, but everything else about us was different. My head was spinning; this was too much.

"Relax," Salem whispered, placing a gentle hand on my shoulder. "It is going to take some adjusting to, but in time, it will all make sense. I promise."

"If you're telling the truth, then why didn't Paul say something before?" I didn't want to believe him but the further I thought about it the more sense it made. I wanted to cry, to scream, to escape. This was all too much in one day.

"He had to wait. It wasn't safe, until now." Salem's blue eyes were serious again and there was no sign of the warm smile he often wore. "Have you ever read about the Salem Witch Trials?"

Why was he suddenly changing the subject? What did this have to do with anything? I nodded slowly, recalling reading about it in middle school.

"Remember how I told you my name was a bit contradictory?"

"Yeah, sure." I remembered it more than I wanted to admit.

"My mother was an ancestor to Alice Young," he spoke quietly, "she was the first witch to be executed during the Trials. Do you understand how this is contradictory?"

"Yes ... " I muttered. "What does this have to do with anything?"

"The world isn't as simple as it might seem, Alexis." He stared out the window behind us. The water rippled elegantly; the bright moonlight reflected upon the lake's surface. "Coincidences simply aren't coincidental."

The cake. The cake wasn't coincidental? On came the spinning again. "What are you trying to tell me, Salem?" I gasped, trying to breathe.

"Calm down," he whispered. "The witches in Massachusetts were real witches."

I shook my head in disbelief. "Are you trying to tell me that you're a witch?"

"Warlock would be the correct term, I suppose," he replied with mild humor, "but no. I'm not a warlock—at least, not exactly."

"Not exactly?" I eyed him suspiciously.

"I have some ... special abilities. Nevertheless, I am definitely not a warlock."

"I think you have a bad case of sleep deprivation or something, Salem. Or you're ... I don't know ... this is insane."

He smirked. "I don't sleep. It isn't necessary for me."

"What?" I laughed, knowing I must still be asleep and suffering from bizarre dreams brought on from the stress of yesterday's events.

"I'll explain that another time."

"I should go home ... " I blurted out suddenly. "This is all wrong. This is all crazy ... you're crazy!"

The last words clearly stung. "I am not crazy. Neither are you. And you are in no condition to be driving right now. You can stay here."

"Here?!" I shouted, bewildered. "Would you stay in some stranger's house after they told you your parents weren't who you thought they were for the past eighteen years, and then told you he had special 'abilities?!'"

Salem frowned, and his eyes reflected the sadness. "Honestly, I probably wouldn't – if I didn't know all of this was true."

● ● ●

My mind was racing with questions and worries, but soon they all seemed to fade. A sense of calm filled me and I felt completely at ease in Salem's presence. "What are these special 'abilities' you claim to have anyway? And how do you do them?"

"That cake." He smiled sheepishly. "I can make things materialize like that."

"What? How?"

"It's a long story, Alexis." He leaned back on the couch. "You probably couldn't handle it all right now. I'll tell you more tomorrow."

"I can handle it," I insisted, although I knew that was a lie. In fact, I was almost certain I was somewhere on the side of the highway, unconscious in my flipped over vehicle and my mind was wandering as I slowly slipped away, because this was impossible. This was not real. *Wake up, Alexis, wake up*! I thought to myself as my mind raced almost as quickly as my heart.

"I won't tell you any more until you have rested", he said firmly. "Would you be more comfortable sleeping on the sofa or in the guest room?"

I wanted to decline both options and yell that I'd prefer to sleep outside in my car, but instead I found myself agreeing to sleep on the couch.

"Good choice. There are much more dangerous things out there to you than me."

It was true that he hadn't hurt me yet, and he had had ample opportunity while I napped earlier.

I didn't object to him helping me stretch out across the sofa, nor did I notice him leave the room to fetch a blanket and pillow. I had to admit that this was comfortable, warm and much better than struggling to sleep in the Alero.

● ● ●

"Goodnight, Alexis, sleep well," Salem whispered as my eyes fell shut uncontrollably. Sleep overcame me quickly as I silently hoped I would wake up in my familiar bed to find this had all truly been a dream.

Paul

There was that familiar tugging again. My dreams were full of wonder, a strange boy named Salem, mom abandoning me ... this time I was more eager to wake up. I was startled when I found myself on a white sofa identical to the one in my dream – or what I had hoped was a dream. I screamed, pulled myself away from the comfortable sectional couch and ran toward the tall milky doors.

As the doors slammed shut behind me, I fell to my knees on the alabaster stairs. My Alero was gone. I fought the urge to scream again, and felt a sudden whip of cold air from behind me.

"Good morning." The silky, sweet voice of the boy from my dream filled my ears.

I rose from the ground and thrust myself at him, my palm prepared to smack him across the cheek, but he was too quick. He gripped my wrist tightly and pulled my arm downward. "There's no need for that." His voice was tense. "Your car isn't gone. It is in the garage."

My eyes fell upon the garage to the left of the house, and I sighed with relief. He released my hand. "While we're out here, why don't we drive over to Paul's business? There are many things he needs to explain to you, and the sooner you know, the sooner you will understand everything," he suggested, his voice calm and gentle now.

"I don't want to go there," I replied stubbornly. If all of this was true, I didn't think I was ready to face reality. Paul *couldn't* be my father.

"You will have to eventually, you know," Salem said calmly. "And somewhere, deep down, you want to."

"What does it matter anyway? It's not like it will change anything."

"It will change a lot of things, actually," he stated. "You'll feel better if you go."

"I highly doubt it."

The garage door opened, revealing my silver car. Salem gripped my hand gently and led me over to the vehicle. Despite all that had happened, it felt strangely good having his hand in mine.

I snapped out of the brief thought of Salem's touch as he pulled my keys from his pocket, holding them in the air between us – the now familiar and alluring smile slightly blocked by the dangling metal. I sighed, taking the keys and climbing into the car. It appeared I had little choice, he was very persistent. I sat behind the steering wheel, pondering whether I could pull out of the garage and go home before he made it into the passenger seat. I put the key in the ignition and started the car, about to put it in reverse when I heard the passenger-side door open and shut.

"You're too slow." He smirked.

"Maybe you're too fast," I said glumly.

After enduring the long winding trip away from Salem's house we finally made it back to town and soon pulled up to Paul's auto shop. I glanced over at Salem, who had an apprehensive look on his face.

"What's the matter with you?" I asked.

His expression changed immediately, although I could tell he was faking the smile this time. "Nothing. Go on ahead, I will wait out here."

"It's fine; I don't care if you come, I mean ... you already know it all anyway, right?" Part of me sincerely wished he would join me; I didn't want to face Paul alone, regardless if I barely knew this boy.

"No." He looked at me sternly. "It would be best if I was not present."

"I really don't think Paul will care if you come with me, if that's what you're worried about."

"I'm staying out here, and that's final," he replied, the fake smile instantly vanishing as he turned away from me.

"Fine!" I said bitterly, slamming the door behind me as I left the boy in the car. His eyes were watchful as I approached the shop. As soon as I opened the glass doors I scrunched my nose. The smell of oil was so overwhelming I had to cup my hand over my nose to keep from gagging.

Paul was nowhere to be seen at first, but I could distinctly hear his voice paired with someone else's. He must have been with a customer. I noticed a small surveillance camera perched high up on the ceiling, and I felt like it was following my every step. It had been years since I came here, but everything looked the same as it always had.

The building wasn't too huge, but large enough to fit a back room full of various-sized car, bicycle and motorcycle tires. There were at least seven aisles of vehicle-related objects that I simply had no idea what were. For me, this was probably the most boring store in existence. Despite that fact, there was nothing else to do other than browse while I waited on my uncle. As I quietly walked down the first aisle, I found a row of things I actually recognized and understood: air fresheners. I picked up a rose-shaped one and sniffed it, displeased by the fact that I could barely smell the scent through the plastic sleeve.

"Can I help you?" a woman's voice asked. I jumped and looked in her direction.

She was about a foot shorter than me – which was unfortunate for her, because I was barely over five feet myself – and a little chunky around the midsection. Her face was round and full, and atop her head was a spiked mess of pink hair. She wore a loose, sleeveless black top that revealed her arms, both of which were covered in vibrant, colorful tattoos. She had to be at least twenty-five or so.

"I-I'm looking for Paul," I stuttered.

"He's with somebody else at the moment. Is there something I can help you with, though?" Her voice was high-pitched and light, bizarre coming from someone of her appearance.

"No. I'm sort of ... family," I wanted to say I was his niece, but I wasn't entirely sure if that was the correct answer anymore.

"Oh!" she grinned and held her hand out, "I'm Kate."

"I'm Alexis," I muttered, wishing I could retreat back to my car and avoid all of this. "Any idea how long until he's done?"

"No idea, but knowing him it could be a while." She laughed. "I think he spends more time buddying up the customers than he does fixing anything."

"What do you do here?" I asked, politely trying to pass the time.

"Me? I work behind the counter," she replied, pointing to the checkout counter at the front of the store.

* * *

"I've been here for almost two years now, and don't tell Paul, but I still don't know jack about half the junk people bring in here."

"Yeah, I've never been much of a car person, either."

Before the pink-haired woman had a chance to say anything else, Paul came walking out from the back of the store grinning and shaking his head. He looked just as I remembered him, if not a little heavier. He was a bulky man, with broad shoulders and muscles fit for a wrestler. His appearance had always intimidated me, but despite the way he looked, he was a gentle man. Atop his head was a thick mane of bronze hair that I was grateful I hadn't inherited from the family gene pool.

"Alex!" he said, walking in our direction with the grin on his face widening more than I thought possible, then suddenly engulfing me in his big arms.

"Hey, Paul," I squeaked under the pressure of his hug.

He released me, the grin never leaving his scruffy, oil-stained face. "Happy birthday!"

I frowned. "I guess *you* wouldn't forget a day like that, huh?"

"What? Forget my favorite niece's birthday?!" He laughed. "What brings you around these parts, having some car troubles? I told your mom that old Al-"

"Mom – no, *Janet* – gave me a letter last night," I interrupted, lying slightly, not mentioning that Salem had filled me in on the rest of the story.

"About what?" he didn't seem to have a clue why I was here. I glanced through the windows at Salem, wondering if it really had all been some sort of elaborate prank. He didn't move an inch.

"About her and Desmond not being ... " The words caught in my throat. "About them not being my real parents."

"Oh ... " he muttered, looking at me in shock. "Do you want to go to the back room?"

I could feel Kate's brown eyes gazing curiously at us. I nodded my head slowly and followed Paul into the back. We were surrounded by boxes of car parts that weren't out on the shelves yet, and in the far corner was a light-brown desk cluttered with used coffee mugs, scattered papers and a checkbook. He took a seat behind the messy desk, and I sat in the seat on the opposite side.

"What exactly did she tell you?" he asked, pushing some of the debris away so he could lean forward with his elbows against the wood top.

"She told me that you are my real ... my real father," I mumbled. "Is it true?"

He appeared just as uncomfortable talking about this as I was. "Yes, Alexis. I am your father." His voice was barely audible.

"Why ... why didn't anyone ever tell me?"

"It was for your own good," he said with a sigh. "I was just trying to protect you."

"Protect me? Protect me from what?"

"From me ... from my lifestyle." He appeared to be having trouble discussing it.

I frowned. "I don't understand, because you're a mechanic or what? Or because you're a single father or something, and you didn't think you could handle raising me alone?"

"That's not it at all ... I'm just not the fatherly type."

"I find that hard to believe." I laughed. "You've always been a good uncle."

● ● ●

"It's much harder than you could understand, Alexis. There's more to it than all that." Paul sighed heavily. "I take it Janet didn't explain much, huh?"

"She didn't really give me much more than 'Paul's your dad!'" It felt wrong lying to Paul about some of the details, but by the way Salem reacted to the idea of even entering the building gave me the feeling that he didn't want Paul knowing he was involved.

He smirked. "That sounds about right for her. This isn't easy for me to tell you ... "

"What isn't?" I was getting impatient; someone needed to give me a straight answer soon before I went insane!

"You are going to think I'm crazy, and you are probably going to want to run away." He stared at me, watching my expression. "But don't. I promise you, there's nothing to run from."

"Get on with it, Paul." I couldn't take any more of these vague answers, between him and Salem, I was getting sick of it.

"The Waldron family is different from ordinary people." He was choosing his words carefully. I barely caught that he said 'Waldron' and not 'Hobbs'. "We are ... vampire hunters."

I burst into laughter, but there was little humor behind what he said. "*Vampire* hunters?" I shook my head, about to get up and leave. "I knew it; it's all a joke. You and Salem are both going to get it for this crap. I-"

"Salem?!" His eyes went from gentle to fierce, almost fearful. "Please tell me it isn't Salem Young."

I opened my mouth to confirm his assumption, but stopped myself. "You're the one who set him up to do it, aren't you? You're obviously both in on it. Okay … you got me!"

"Alexis, this is serious." Paul growled. "Salem Young isn't safe."

"He seems perfectly safe, and friendly, to me," I objected.

"Alexis, this is not a damned joke. I'm being serious!" I somehow knew by the tone in his voice and the look in his eyes that everything I had been told was indeed true. "Salem … he's one of them!"

"One of … them?" I gulped. "Them? As in a 'vampire'?"

Paul nodded slowly. "He's one of the ones that lives around these parts that I haven't been able to kill yet."

"You kill people!" I gasped in horror.

"They aren't *people*, Alex. They're monsters!"

"I don't believe in monsters."

"Please, you have to listen to me," he pleaded, reaching across the table to touch my hand. I pulled away.

"So, why did Janet and Desmond pretend for so long, how are they involved?"

"They don't know the full truth," he said quietly. "I put you in foster care after your mother passed away, hoping someone would find you and give you a better life than I could ever offer here on my own. But, I insisted they let me be a part of your life. So, I played the role of your uncle. You can't imagine how hard it was, pretending all of this time to be your uncle," he explained with grief. "I told Janet that by the time you were old enough, I wanted you to know the truth about where you came from. I guess eighteen is old enough to understand in her book. All she knew, though, is that I was your dad, and that your real mom passed away."

"Why did it have to wait until now?"

"I had to protect you from them, if they knew I had a young daughter ... " He shook his head. "There's no telling what they might have done to you. It was for the best. But now you're older, stronger, and more able to understand all this. Hell, you might even turn out to be a fine hunter."

"I refuse to believe this, Paul! It's not funny anymore." I didn't know what to think, my head was spinning with everything Paul and Salem and said.

I got up from my chair, ignoring his pleading calls and left the room. Tears began to stream down my cheek, from frustration and confusion. Then I looked out the window to see Salem in my car, staring back at me. I walked slowly out of the auto shop and grasped the handle to my door. I was scared to open it, afraid that Paul hadn't been joking ... but the welcoming smile on Salem's flawless face made me change my mind. I collapsed onto my seat and glanced over at him cautiously.

I thought over everything that I had read in vampire novels—noting the fact that he was out here, in the sunlight, not burning to a crisp. However, he *was* breathtakingly beautiful, and he did have a pallid complexion, but he seemed harmless—aside from the bizarre episode about his 'special abilities' that he went on about. Crazy ... but harmless.

Salem opened his mouth to speak, but I put my hand up to stop him as I remembered what Paul had said. "There's more about you than you let on last night isn't there? You're not just some far-off offspring of a witch, are you?"

He lowered his eyes. "You are correct, Alexis Waldron."

Waldron. "Why didn't you tell me?"

"I was afraid of how you would react."

"But if you are what Paul says you are, and you try to avoid this place, why would you want to bring me here?"

Salem sighed. "I promised Janet I would."

"How's my mom ... Janet ... involved in any of this?"

"She knows my secret," he spoke quietly. "All thanks to Mark."

"Mark? As in her boyfriend?"

He nodded. "He is one of us as well."

"What?! Oh my god, is she in danger?!" I asked, beyond alarmed. Regardless if she was my biological mom or not, I still loved her.

"Of course she isn't." He smiled reassuringly.

"This is all some sort of trick, right?" My voice was filled with panic as I stared at him with pleading eyes. "Tell me this isn't real. Tell me my mom is at home waiting for me, and that she's secretly planning a surprise party and is just using you guys to distract me."

"I wish I could," Salem replied.

"I don't know what to think. This is all impossible," I said, shaking my head. "Okay, I'll play along Mr. Vampire, but I have one question."

"Anything."

"Why, if Paul is your enemy, are you willing to be around me at all? Aren't you afraid hunting is in my blood or something? Or that, you know ... *HE* might kill you?"

"I told you before. I find you intriguing; in more ways than I can even explain. And, you haven't been taught in the ways of hunting; therefore, I have nothing to fear from you. As far as Paul goes, I have nothing to worry about."

"Nothing to worry about? I have another one for you, then. If you're a vampire, how are you out here in the sun? Shouldn't you have shriveled up and died by now? Or burst into flame?"

He grimaced. "This is reality, Alexis, not a story. Everything you have read about vampires—most of it is inaccurate or downright false. We are not beautiful; we don't turn into bats; we don't shrivel up in the sunlight, and we are most definitely not afraid of something as fickle as *garlic*."

"That's not entirely true," I whispered bashfully, turning to look out the window, hoping he somehow had not heard.

"What isn't?" he questioned.

"The beautiful part," I said, turning back to look at him.

"You are too kind." The sound of his laugh extinguished my embarrassment.

"So, then it is all true?" I paused for a moment. "Are you going to kill me?" I really wished I didn't always blurt out what I was thinking.

He put his finger on my chin and turned my face toward him. I flinched at his touch, trembling slightly. "I would never hurt you. In fact, I have no interest in hurting anyone else for that matter."

"Paul said you're a monster, and that I shouldn't trust you."

"Paul," he said through gritted teeth, "is the monster. A lot of vampires haven't done anything wrong, not in a very long time. Some of us haven't at all. The hunters ... the ones that kill without feeling or discrimination ... they are the monsters!"

"A long time? So you're saying you used to be a monster?" I asked.

"Some of us, yes. Some still are, but I'm not among those. These hunters such as Paul do not understand that many of us are different. They only judge us by what we are, not who we are."

I stared into his pale blue eyes, wondering if he was telling the truth. If he really was a vampire, there was no telling over how many years he could have perfected the art of lying. "If your kind is nothing to be afraid of, why do hunters even exist?"

"I said a lot of us, not all of us. There are some vampires that are still a definite threat to society, and that is why the Waldron lineage exists. Your ancestors are natural-born hunters of our kind. It would overwhelm you to know just how many vampires exist in the world, how many exist in just this little town. That is why hunters exist."

I gulped at his words, trying to avoid wondering just how many vampires were roaming around in what I thought to be a peaceful little town. Sure, Willowshire wasn't perfect—we had criminals just as any town did, but thinking that there were undead monsters roaming through the city sounded far more sinister than your everyday crook. "Are your special abilities a part of being ... what you are?"

"No," he said quietly. "I have always assumed it was something to do with my father's heritage."

"Your last name is kind of contradictory, too," I said, speaking my thoughts again. "That is, assuming all those vampire stories are true – and that you have been a vampire for a long time ... " I was prepared to ramble, but he stopped me.

He smirked. "I suppose you are right. However, how did you know that I'm not as young as you are?"

"The way you talk and dress, your love for classical music and books, and maybe a little that you can't drive a car." I laughed.

"Those are all very valid reasons," he replied "Of course, how ancient must *you* be to love classical music and books as well?"

"Ha! That has nothing to do with how old I am."

We laughed for a couple of minutes, but I stopped abruptly and glanced at him. "Well, how old are you?"

"I was born in 1885," he replied, bracing himself in assumption that I would freak out.

"You're 126?" I gaped at him, quickly doing the math in my head.

"More or less." He shrugged. "It's hard to keep track after all of this time. After a couple dozen, they start to blend together."

I glanced up toward the auto shop window and saw Paul glaring out at us. I wondered if he could see Salem despite the glare on my windshield.

"We should probably get out of here ... " I muttered and Salem followed my gaze.

"Let's go to your house," he said quickly.

"Why would we go there?" I asked as I pulled out of the parking lot.

"Don't you want to?"

"I guess ... " I sighed as I turned left onto the road. "Not like there's anything there for me now, though."

"All of your belongings are there."

"Yeah. That's it."

"It will make you feel better," he assured me, but I was certain it would do the opposite. Nevertheless, I agreed to go home ... at least temporarily.

Black Bears

The house was cold, vacant and depressing. I wanted to run to my room, collapse onto my bed and sleep until this nightmare was over. Salem followed me inside, although uninvited, admiring his surroundings as we passed through the kitchen and into the living room. It was incredibly dull and shabby in contrast to his house. I groaned when I smelled the sour milk that had spilled across the dining room floor the prior morning. I quickly gathered the mop and cleaned it up, spraying the area with cleaner to eliminate the wretched smell.

"You never did explain to me how you afford to live in that mansion of yours," I commented as I watched him look at my place.

"It is hardly a mansion, and technically, I did," he said as he looked at the TV set. "I told you I can make things materialize at will."

"So you're telling me you created a whole house?" I said sarcastically.

He laughed lightly. "No, of course I didn't. The house was abandoned when I arrived here, barely more than a rotting hull. The furniture and touch-ups, however ... "

"How do you do it?" He was still fascinated by the TV. I grabbed the remote off of the boring, scratched up brown coffee table.

"Magic." He grinned up at me.

I glared. "I'm serious, tell me how?"

"I think of something, and it appears. It is really simple."

"*Anything*?"

"No. I can materialize a wide variety of objects. The smaller they are, the easier it is for me. I definitely could never manage anything as large as a house. And it's not something I am in constant control of."

"What do you mean?"

"I only discovered the ability a few years ago, and sometimes it works ... other times, not so much." He laughed somewhat to himself. "Initially, things sort of backfired. For example, if I were to imagine a lamp ... it would come out disfigured and broken. I eventually figured it out, though."

"And what happened when you first figured out you could do this ... magic?"

"Well, I was ... startled, as anyone would be." He appeared to be deep in thought. "But considering who and what I am, it didn't affect me as much as it may would others, I suppose."

I hit the power button on the TV remote and a news report spread across the 32' screen. Salem jumped back.

"Please tell me you've at least seen a TV before."

"I'm 126 years-old Alexis, of course I have seen a television." He shook his head at me. "I just wasn't expecting it to come on."

• • •

I wasn't paying attention at this point; I was watching the TV intently. The slick-haired man behind the screen was talking about an incident in Denver, Colorado. My heart was beating rapidly as I stared. I hardly noticed Salem walk up beside me.

"What is it?" he asked, watching the screen.

I tuned out his voice and heard only the rough voice of the news reporter.

"Earlier today at the Denver Zoo, a black bear escaped its holding pens while a zookeeper was placing food in its enclosure," he spoke quickly, "the woman was found brutally attacked within the bear's exhibit. We are still unsure how the bear escaped."

My heart sunk as a picture of a woman was pulled up on the screen. "No!" I screamed.

Salem's voice reached my ears again. "Alexis ... " It was merely a gentle whisper, right behind my ear.

"No! Don't you dare to speak to me or touch me!" I shouted, pushing him away. "Mark did this! I know it!"

He looked taken aback by my assumption. "You think Mark did this?" He frowned. "We aren't like that, Alexis. There is no evidence that he had any involvement. The reporter clearly said that it was a bear attack."

"That doesn't make him innocent! It could all be some sort of cover up!"

"You are just upset because he took her from you."

"That has nothing to do with it!" Or did it? It was more Paul's fault than Mark's wasn't it? I fell back on the sofa. "Did it say ... did it say if she was still alive?"

"I didn't hear anything about her dying." He sat beside me on the faux leather couch. "I assure you; it has nothing to do with Mark."

"I won't believe it until I hear it from mom – Janet, I mean." Not calling her mom was going to take a while to get used to.

"Why don't you call her?" he suggested.

"Right," I nodded, relaxing just a little as I stood up and got the cordless phone from the kitchen. So much for crude accusations the first time I called her after she left. I dialed her cell phone number. It rang once. Twice. Three times.

"Hello?" A deep male's voice answered.

"Is Janet there?" I said.

"She can't come to the phone right now. Who is this?"

"This is her daughter," I said, ignoring the fact that I wasn't really her daughter anymore ... or never was, I supposed. "Please, just put her on the phone."

"She's a little out of it right now, but I'll see if she is able."

"Thank you," I said.

Silence followed, and then muffled voices in the background.

"Alexis?" Her voice was different, scared, weak. "I was about to have Mark call you."

"How are you?" I felt relieved to hear her voice, but something about the way she spoke made me uneasy.

"I have been better." I heard her laugh, which was cut through with a hoarse cough and groan. "Happy birthday, sweetie."

"Thanks, mom ... " I muttered. "Tell me what happened."

I heard the muffled voice of Mark in the background, but I couldn't decipher what he was saying. "I was feeding the brown bears, when one of them must have gotten loose-"

* * *

I broke her off suddenly. "The person on the news said black bears."

"Right ... " she trailed off. "Black bears. My mind is a bit hazy right now."

"Did Mark do something to you?" I blurted out anxiously.

"Of course not!" Her voice sounded unconvincing, almost as anxious as my own, "He's right here with me in the hospital, making sure I'm taken care of."

"How badly were you hurt, are you going to be okay?"

"It's not as bad as the TV might make it sound. It's just a few scratches really."

"The news reporter said you were brutally injured."

"The TV was over-exaggerating, like they always do. You know that." I heard another bout of coughing then Janet's voice was replaced by the deep male again. "Janet needs her rest. I'll have her call you back when she is feeling better."

He hung up. I crumbled onto the sofa, bawling my eyes out in frustration.

"What did she say?" Salem asked tenderly as he sat beside me.

I filled him in on the entire conversation, including the errors in her story. It must have been difficult to comprehend through my sobs.

"Perhaps she is just hazy like she said ... " he said with the faintest hint of doubt in his voice.

"You don't believe it any more than I do, do you?" I said, sitting up and looking into his eyes.

He looked down, strands of black falling across his face. "I believe that Mark was in no way responsible for this."

"I need to go to her," I said suddenly, angrily. Was no one on my side today?

"No, you don't. Everything will be fine, trust me."

"Trust you?! I don't even know you!"

"Alexis, you need to calm down. Relax."

"Calm down?! First, my mom left me, then I find out all this unbelievable crap about Paul and vampires, and now my mom is lying in some hospital bed with some monster supposedly watching over her!"

"Even if it were true about Mark, you wouldn't be able to do anything."

"I could help her!"

"No, you couldn't. And besides ... you are too important to risk, regardless my insistence on Mark's goodness."

"Important? You barely even know me, Salem!"

"As far as you know," he whispered.

"What are you even talking about?"

"I can't explain it right now." He sighed. "Your friends are expecting you to be bright and cheerful."

"What?"

"It's your birthday, remember?" He attempted a grin. "They're coming over to celebrate."

"How do you know?"

He shrugged his shoulders. "That blonde-haired girl might have mentioned it."

"Of course she did ... " I grumbled. "Is this the real reason you wanted me to come home so badly?"

"That might have played some part in it, yes."

Happy Birthday

     Salem remained downstairs in the living room while I took a quick shower before my visitors arrived. I changed out of my blue jeans and red tank top into a flowing dark-blue skirt and white, semi-frilly sleeveless shirt. I felt a little over-dressed, but it was my birthday party after all, so why not. Time passed slowly as I waited for the guests to arrive, and Salem was sitting silently on the sofa staring off into space. I wondered what was on his mind, but before I had the chance to question him, someone hammered their fist against the door. Salem came out of his stupor at once and stood up.

     I peeked through the tiny peephole and groaned. There were at least ten of my classmates waiting out there. After putting on a false smile, I reluctantly twisted the door knob and let them flood into my house. They piled their presents on the dining room table and wished me a happy birthday individually. I was surprised not to see Jason or Karen among the crowd.

     "Karen told me to tell you she'd be a little late," Brittany Crosswood said casually, as if answering my unspoken question. She was more of Karen's friend than my own. In fact, most of these people were little more than acquaintances, despite being in the same room as most of them for countless hours.

"Ah, okay," I said quietly. Someone turned on the old, black stereo that sat on the end table beside the sofa and started blaring music. I sighed.

Jason showed up about five minutes later, bustling in through the door without knocking and heaving a gift at me with a grin. The present was flat and badly wrapped. "Open it!"

"Now?" I asked, rattling the present around. "Shouldn't we wait until I open the other presents too?"

"Nah, no one's going to care," he insisted.

"Okay ... " I pulled at the paper and gasped in shock when I realized what it was. I gaped at the sleek, black laptop that I held in my hands, temporarily speechless. "Oh, Jace! This is too much!" I flung my arms around his muscular form in a tight hug.

He laughed happily. "You've been saying for so long that you wanted one, so I've been secretly saving up my allowance and money from the part-time job at Howard's."

Howard's was a small convenience store in town that Jason had worked at for the past five months or so. I could feel them coming, the warmth of tears building up in my eyes. I fought them, but I wasn't strong enough. Not today. I hugged him tightly again. "You shouldn't have ... " I whispered.

"I wanted to," he said with a grin. "Besides, after what you've been through, I'm extra glad I decided to do it. You needed some excitement, after ... well, you know —all that."

If only he knew just how much I had gone through. I finally released him and happily ran to my room to put away my new laptop. As I headed back down the stairs, I saw the front door whip open and Karen came waltzing in carrying what was unmistakably a cake box. I smiled and approached her.

"Happy birthday, Alex!" she shouted when she saw me. "You look so much better than when you left school. I was worried sick, really."

"I feel a lot better too, and thanks ... I will be okay," I lied; the excitement from the computer had been enough to mask the stress on my face, for now. "So, what kind of cake did you get?"

I pictured the cheesecake Salem had summoned for me last night, knowing that this one would not compare. "It's just chocolate with vanilla frosting. It's not very exciting, I know ... but I didn't know what to get. I figured this was the safest bet with so many people here. And I mean, if you don't like chocolate, you can get out! Right?"

"That's right!" We both laughed, and for the briefest of moments, everything else melted away temporarily.

"So he didn't come, huh?"

"What? Who?"

"That new boy from school. I saw him like, right after you told us about him. He's got a cruuush on you, I think," she said teasingly.

"He didn't?" I said as I glanced into the living room, expecting to see him sitting down on the sofa again, but instead seeing a room full of people dancing to the beat of an unrecognizable song playing on the radio. I could barely imagine what it would be like when Jason threw his party – I knew way more than ten people would be showing up for that one.

"Let me handle this," Karen said in disgrace when she saw my face. I watched her casually enter the living room and shut off the radio. "How about everyone gets ready for Alex to open her presents while I order us some pizza?"

Everyone settled down after cheering at the idea of pizza. I smiled thankfully at my blonde friend as she passed by to order the food. The crowd of teenagers deserted the living room and filled the small dining area, surrounding me and the table of unopened gifts. Karen joined them after hanging up the phone.

"You've got to open mine first!" she insisted, handing me a small white gift bag.

I knew no matter what anyone got me, it wouldn't compare to the laptop from Jason. I opened the bag to reveal a gift card to Karen's favorite clothes store. I smiled, despite my disappointment. A gift card to almost anywhere else would have suited me better, but she was always insistent on me changing my style. Chances were that this would only end up lost somewhere, never used—but it was the thought that counted, I suppose.

Next was a present from Mitchell Banner, Jason's younger brother. It was a simple card with ten dollars in it—fine with me; money was almost always my favorite choice of gift—I could get whatever I really wanted that way. I shot him a smile and said 'thank you' before tearing open the next gift. As the pile dwindled down to the very last one, I had a mass of random things before me that I didn't need or necessarily want, but was, nevertheless, thankful for.

"Who is that one from?" Karen asked curiously, pointing at the last remaining present.

The last gift on the table was neatly wrapped in shining teal paper. I eyed it suspiciously, having not seen anyone bring it in. As I picked it up, I felt my heartbeat quicken when I read the tag: 'From Salem.'

"It's from him ... " I said quietly.

* * *

"Who? That boy?! So he is here?" Her voice grew excited as she glanced around the room.

"I-I don't know," I said honestly, wondering where he had escaped to.

I tore open the paper, and my jaw dropped. It was an entire collection of Edgar Allan Poe's work in a beautiful leather-bound book, identical to the one Janet had left behind. There was a thin piece of paper, roughly the size of a bookmark, sticking up between the pages. I flipped through the book and pulled out the paper. In beautifully scripted letters, it read '*To my little raven.*', and it was placed on the page where *The Raven* began. I felt my cheeks grow warm. I shut the book hastily as Karen came creeping over to peek over my shoulder.

"Well, what is it?" she asked impatiently.

"It's just a book."

"That's lame. Who gets someone homework for their birthday?" She laughed.

I glared at her. "It was a very thoughtful gift!" The words came out angrier than I had intended.

Karen looked taken aback, and I frowned. "I'm sorry," I apologized. "I'm just stressed ... from you know what."

She nodded slowly. "I understand." I wondered if she really did. "But I mean if this boyfriend of yours is trying to impress you, he should've gotten you some jewelry!"

I smacked her on the shoulder playfully. "Boyfriend? I hardly know him!"

"Uh-huh, and what was all that blushing about then? Huh?"

Before I could muster a response, I was saved by a knock on the door. The pizza delivery man arrived and carried in four large pizza boxes. As everyone gathered plates of food, I stood back and waited. There were only two slivers of plain cheese pizza left by the time I got to the boxes. I wasn't surprised that no one had been considerate enough to let me, the birthday girl, get her share first. Nor did I really care; I wanted this all to be over with – And I wanted to know where Salem had gone to.

I sat alone in the living room on the sofa while everyone else chattered in the dining area, downing bite after bite of pizza.

"Cake time!" Karen shouted and dragged me out of the living room.

Good. This meant the facade was almost over, and I could go to bed. She lit eighteen brightly-colored candles, and the whole room was filled with a chorus of the traditional birthday song. I smiled awkwardly as everyone sung, noting that Mitchell was only moving his lips to the words and not really singing, then I blew out the candles. Karen dished out slices of cake to everyone—giving me the first slice this time. At least someone was being considerate. I smiled gratefully before sulking back to my spot on the couch.

She joined me moments later, followed by Jason. "So, how do you like the party, Alex?" she asked as she put a forkful of chocolate cake into her mouth.

I shrugged my shoulders as I swallowed. "So far, so good." I smiled.

"That's good. I hope it isn't too much ... I just thought you would feel better with some company."

"I know. I appreciate it, really."

"Admit it – you're in a hurry to get all of these people out of here so you can play with your new toy." Jason winked at me.

"If by new toy, you mean that boy ... " Karen laughed.

"I told you, I don't even know him!" For a moment, I thought about what it would be like to be with a vampire but quickly shook the notion away. I had never been all that interested in having a boyfriend, anyway.

"Wait, what? Alex has a boyfriend?" Jason said, more than a little shocked.

"No, she's just talking about that new boy from music class I told you guys about in the gym.""

"Oh right, him. Come on Karen, Alex wouldn't be into some music nerd." He laughed and Karen followed suit.

"You guys know me way too well," I lied, though not sure why. It was better to just leave it at that and get this night over with, besides, the thought of Salem and I together was preposterous.

They both laughed again then returned to eating their cake. To my relief, the rest of the guests were already leaving. A few of them wished me a happy birthday again before vanishing out of the front door. Mitchell stayed behind to give me a quick hug and tell Jason that he was going to walk home. I sighed with relief and leaned back on the sofa.

"Thanks, again, both of you," I said, stifling a yawn.

"No problem," Karen said proudly. "Do you want me to stay and help clean up?"

"No, it's fine. I can handle it."

"Let me know how the laptop runs," Jason said.

"I will!" I said cheerfully and embraced him again. "I still can't believe you spent all of that time and money."

"It's not a big deal, really." He smiled. "Just make sure to put it to good use."

"Oh, I will for sure."

I followed them both to the door, quickly saying good-bye and sharing a warm group hug before they walked off to Jason's car. I wasn't surprised that they were leaving together, considering we were all three really close. I sighed with relief when I closed the door, then nearly screamed when I felt the cold skin against my arm. Turning around slowly, I lowered my guard.

"I didn't mean to startle you," Salem said apologetically.

"Where have you been?" I gasped.

"Upstairs," he replied casually. "I figured I would give you some privacy."

"You could have stayed."

"It would have caused a scene."

"No it wouldn't have," I replied, but he was probably right. Everyone would be wondering who he was – and who knows what Karen or Jason would have done. "Thank you so much for the book, by the way."

"It was my pleasure." He smiled. "I hope you don't mind."

"Why would I? I love it."

"Well, what I mean to say is, I hope you don't mind that I used the blank book Janet sent you."

"How did you do that?" I blinked.

"The same way I summon all other objects ... I wasn't sure if I would be able to do it, but I think it worked as planned."

I grabbed the book off the table, turning the crisp pages and noting that everything was exactly as I remembered reading it in other volumes. I plucked the paper out from the book and examined it. "I don't mind; I hadn't planned to use the book as a diary or anything, anyway. How did you know this was my favorite story?" I asked quietly, turning the thin piece of paper in my hand.

"Good guess?" he grinned. "Plus, it is hardly a surprise, considering your last name."

"Hobbs?" I wondered.

"No, *Waldron*," he corrected. "Hobbs isn't your surname, after all, remember?"

"Right ... " I had sort of spaced that fact out. "What does that have to do with anything, though?"

"Waldron translates into the word 'wall-raven', which in a roundabout way is said to mean 'strong raven'," he said – that explained the little note scrawled across the bookmark.

"Oh," I said, considering what it could possibly mean ... probably nothing. "How do you know that?"

"I have done my research," he explained calmly. "You aren't going to like this, but your family is sort of my mortal enemies."

"Emphasis on 'mortal', right?" I laughed half-heartedly. "How is it they haven't ... killed you. I mean ... considering they seem to know you are here, and Paul said you're one of the few he hasn't been able to finish off?"

"I'm smarter than they anticipate." Salem shrugged. "Plus, I don't go looking for trouble like some of my kind do. Some vampires enjoy the thrill of being hunted. God only knows why."

"How come I've never heard about real vampires before? I mean, if there are so many of you out there it would be all over the place. Nothing's a secret these days."

"We ... they ... don't act out in the open; they are discreet about what they do. Most likely, a lot of the murder stories you see on the news or read in the newspaper are related to vampires."

I frowned, not liking where this was going. "Do you ... " I paused, unsure of what to say.

He seemed to understand and smiled reassuringly at me. "Of course not."

"Then, what do you do about blood? I mean, that part of being a vampire is true, isn't it?"

He shut his eyes briefly and sighed. "I was hoping to avoid these questions. Yes, that much is true. It is simple ... there are other ways to satisfy my needs, such as through animal blood."

"Oh." I walked to the kitchen counter and collected the empty pizza boxes. "You weren't born this way, right?" I asked as I went to the front door.

Salem opened the door and followed me out. "No, I was once an ordinary human," he said with obvious remorse.

I dumped the boxes into the large green trash can beside my house. Moments later, I brought out a trash bag full of discarded wrapping paper, paper plates and the empty cake box.

"Well, how did you become a vampire, then?" I asked as we went back indoors. Salem was quiet for a while, thinking I guessed.

"My memory is foggy, as bizarre as that might sound. I believe that is how it is for all of us – perhaps we repress the memories, although maybe it is just due to how long it has been," he eventually replied, sitting beside me on the sofa. "From what I can recall, the place I called home had caught fire one night ... there was smoke everywhere, my sister was screaming ... I never heard my mother or father, but I could distinctly hear Hannah somewhere in the house. I can vaguely recall seeing her, but I'm not sure what happened to her ... " He paused; I could see the sorrow in his eyes as the images replayed through his mind.

"She was barely three at that point. I made it out of the house before it crumbled completely, but I didn't escape completely unscathed. I suffered severe burns across my lower half. Raziel – my 'Sire', the man who bit me—claims that he found me in the alley behind my house, writhing in agony ... instead of putting my misery to an end, he elongated it for the next 120 years or so." he scowled.

"You are miserable?" I frowned as I stared into his pale eyes.

"Well ... not at the moment." He looked back at me. "The pain of becoming ... what I am ... was beyond anything you could ever imagine, for so many different reasons. My chance at living a normal life was taken away from me that night," he muttered in anguish. "But, at the same time, had it not been for that, I would have been dead centuries ago. Although watching the world grow and expand has been a gift, the rest of what you have to endure isn't worth it.

"I lost my family, not only to the fire, but to becoming what I am. My friends, I couldn't see them ever again. Everything was taken away from me that night. Everyone I knew and loved eventually aged, withered away and died, while I was cursed to walk this Earth alone for eternity – watching it all unfold from a distance."

I wondered if vampires were able to cry as I stared at him, but no tears came. The need to comfort him overcame me, but I didn't know how. "I'm so sorry, Salem ... " I whispered, trying to ignore the growing curiosity to ask even more questions.

"Don't be." He smiled and placed his cold hand against my cheek. "If none of that had happened, I would never have met you."

I laughed. "Don't forget you're talking to the offspring of a vampire hunter."

Salem just smiled. I admired his expression for far too long; I lowered my gaze and blushed. "Can I ask one more question?"

"Anything."

"What happened to this Raziel guy?"

"He still exists somewhere, as far as I know. For the first five years of my 'new life', as he called it, he treated me as a slave. Although, he referred to me as his "apprentice," I felt like nothing more than a servant. He taught me the ways of being a vampire, but it sickened me. I refused to indulge in human blood, knowing I had once been one – my family were humans, my friends. I would never have done that to them, why would I even consider doing that to anyone?" He flinched at the idea. "He would have me bring him ... food ... every night." The pained look on his face was almost unbearable.

"People?" I gasped, knowing the answer.

He grimaced. "I wouldn't have felt quite as miserable had it been criminals or terminally ill beings ... but these were innocent people."

"How could you put up with that for so long?"

"I had no other options, or so I thought," he grumbled. "You weren't the only one who fell for the lore of vampires. Raziel tried to convince me the stories were all true, that if I went out in the daytime I would combust." His eyes darkened. "One specific night, he made me do something intolerable. I couldn't bear to exist after that ... He requested I bring him 'young blood', as he called it. In other words, the blood of a child – Raziel said it was the tastiest, most invigorating blood imaginable. I had no choice but to obey him, at least that's what I thought at the time.

"She couldn't have been much older than Hannah had been. I snuck through her nursery window, plucked her from her crib and presented her to Raziel. I immediately regretted what I had done. The next morning, I decided to end myself. It came down to either spending eternity doing his bidding or risking my existence by stepping out into the sunlight. I braced myself for death as I stepped out into the morning light, anticipating the inevitable —but it never came." I noticed how he never referred to it as his 'life'. "I stood out in the sun for at least fifteen minutes, and nothing happened." He stopped abruptly and changed the subject. "You should try calling Janet again, before it gets too late."

I blinked, deep in thought as I tried to imagine what he had been through. I couldn't imagine what it would be like to not only never talk to my best friends again, but to watch them grow old and die while I remained young. "Yeah, you're right ... "

I grabbed the cordless phone, sat cross-legged on the sofa and dialed the familiar number. I only waited through two rings this time before her familiar voice answered.

"Hey mom," I said into the receiver. Would I ever be able to stop calling her that? "I just wanted to make sure you were all right."

"I'm getting there." She sounded better, happier than our last conversation at the least. "How was your birthday?"

"It wasn't as bad as I thought it'd be." I laughed. "Karen threw me a surprise party, which went okay. Jason got me a laptop!"

"That's great, sweetie!" I heard the muffled voice in the background. "I have to go; my dinner is getting cold. Go enjoy the rest of your night."

"Okay, keep in touch. Okay?"

"I will. Don't worry too much."

"I'll try. Bye, mom." It might be impossible to call her anything but that.

"Bye, sweetie."

Salem delicately took the phone from my grasp and sat it on the coffee table. "You have more questions," he said knowingly.

"Just a couple," I replied shyly. "What happened to the burns?"

"Becoming a vampire could be seen as a type of cleansing, I suppose. Any illness, wound, scar, or deformity you might have had as a human is healed upon turning."

"Then, in a sense, isn't it better to become a vampire?"

"No!" he shouted, causing me to look away in slight regret for asking. "*Nothing* is worth this sort of existence."

"Okay," I croaked. "One more thing ... " I braced myself for anger, but instead received a smile.

"Ask away," he said gingerly.

"It's more of a fact than a question." I twiddled my thumbs nervously. "Your eyes – they change color when you're summoning things or whatever ... "

He blinked. "You noticed that?"

"Yes ... "

"I am impressed." He smirked. "You must be very observant."

"Not usually," I confessed. "What else can you tell me about vampires? I want to know everything." I was surprised by my own question, but I had grown genuinely interested in the topic.

"While some of what you have heard or read or seen are definite myths, there are some attributes we definitely do obtain—such as speed. We can run quicker than any human, and drinking the blood of humans makes us exceptionally strong," he looked disgusted for a mere moment. "Powerful vampires can possess the ability to share visions and memories with others by the mere touch of their hand. I spent many years experimenting with what I could and could not do after I left Raziel. It truly was amazing to me that daylight did not kill me, and I wondered what else was and was not true.

● ● ●

"I knew that sleeping was no longer necessary, but I attempted to sleep, nevertheless—simply because Raziel claimed it was impossible, and I was stubborn enough to put it to the test. Unfortunately, he was correct. I cannot even imagine what dreaming is like anymore." He sighed and looked at me. "That's enough vampire talk for now though, I think."

"Surely there is more that you can tell me." I was practically begging. Perhaps it was the vampire hunter in me that hungered for more information, or maybe I was just a curious girl.

"Well, there is one thing," he said with an expression of discomfort. "But I would really prefer not to discuss it right now."

My eyebrows arched upward. "Now you *have* to tell me."

"I am afraid that it might upset you, Alexis."

Swallowing hard, I tried to keep my face straight. "Why would it upset me?"

"Because I used this particular ability on you."

"What ... what are you talking about, Salem?"

"Vampires are able to persuade mortals into doing essentially anything, without even a single motion."

My eyes were firmly locked on him, my mouth agape and an involuntary shudder rippled down my spine. "That's how you convinced me to agree to stay at your place?"

"That's how I convinced you to come to my house. The effect was beginning to wear off towards the end of the evening, hence your outburst in the morning."

It was difficult to restrain myself from feeling angry. I felt completely violated, yet at the same time there was a part of me that was thankful that I'd gone with him and learned what I had. Now I understood why I kept having conflicted feelings about it, and the sudden calmness I'd felt after wanting to panic and leave. "Promise me you'll never use it on me again."

"I promise," he vowed.

The room fell silent for a moment, and then Salem glanced up at the clock. It was nearing 10pm. "Do you need to go somewhere?" I asked, trying to avoid thinking about this new-found knowledge.

"No," he replied. "I was just noticing your birthday is coming to an end."

"I don't mind." I laughed. "Not this year."

"There was one last gift I wanted to give you, but I wasn't sure how you would react." He looked uneasy.

"What is it?" I asked anxiously.

"It would be easier for me to show you, than to tell you."

I eyed him suspiciously. "Are you going to summon something out of thin air again or something?"

"No, not exactly." He chuckled. "Alexis, I know it is hard for you to fathom right now, but you do mean a lot to me."

"Yeah, you keep saying that. Are you ever going to explain what you're talking about?"

"In due time." He smiled lightly. "Close your eyes."

I hesitated a moment before letting my eyelids fall shut. My heart was thumping wildly in my chest as I waited intently for whatever was coming. Maybe he had lied about not being enticed by human blood and was about to bite into my throat; oddly part of me didn't care. My eyes almost flew open as I felt Salem's cool breath against the side of my face. Tenderly, he brushed his cold lips against my cheek.

"Happy birthday, Alexis," he whispered into my ear.

I was speechless, breathless ... *breathless*. "Salem ... " I became more focused. "You can breathe?"

"Not quite as literally as you can," he replied, obviously stunned by my unexpected response to his action.

"Oh." My expression was blank momentarily, and then I grinned at him. "I was wrong earlier when I thought to myself nothing could compare to the laptop Jason gave me."

His lips twisted into a magnificent smile before he stood up. I was uncertain what he was doing at first, until he pried me off of the sofa and effortlessly cradled me in his arms as he made his way up the stairs. I grasped his arms tightly, afraid with every step that he would drop me. Somewhere deep inside I also still feared for my blood. What if he couldn't control his hunger around me?

We approached my bedroom door, which was wide open and inviting. He laid me gracefully across my soft mattress and pulled the covers up over me. I nearly objected before he put a cold finger to my lips.

"It's late, and you have had a long, tiresome day," he whispered. "Get some sleep."

"But I haven't even gotten to enjoy my presents yet!" I playfully whined.

"Not even the last one?" he asked with an innocent grin.

"Well, when you put it that way ... I enjoyed one of my gifts." I yawned. I was more tired than I had realized.

"Goodnight," he whispered sweetly and I drifted away into a deep slumber, thinking how maybe it wasn't so preposterous to imagine Salem and I as a couple.

Destiny

My dreams were filled with horrific images. A raven hovered over a burning house. Shrill screams of an infant. Salem, covered head to toe in flames, wobbling helplessly out of the smoldering building. A dark, cloaked figure whisking him up from the gray cobblestone alleyway. I heard him screaming, saw him writhing in agony.

"Alex!" Salem's voice yelled my name as the figure pressed his lips against the base of his neck. The world started to quiver and shake, and I heard him call my name again.

My eyes flew open. Salem was shaking me, yelling my name. "You were screaming in your sleep ... are you okay?" he asked as he saw my eyes were open.

"I-I think so." I clung onto his cold, thin body. "It was horrible." I sobbed into his shoulder.

"It was only a dream," he said reassuringly.

"It was a *nightmare*, about you ... " I muttered. "The burning house, Hannah, Raziel ... and then I heard your voice calling for me."

"That part wasn't a dream," he replied.

• • •

"There was a bird, too." I remembered suddenly. "It was flying over the burning building … a raven."

Salem flinched. "Raziel claimed that some hunters could transform into ravens."

"Are … are Waldron's the only vampire hunters?"

"Surely not, the world is a vast place, but the Waldron's are the only ones I have ever directly encountered." He stared at me inquisitively. "Maybe you should speak to Paul again. Ask him if he knows anything about that ability."

"How would he know?"

"He knows a lot about vampire and hunter history alike. However, don't tell him I sent you … he can't know that I am with you. In fact, it's best that no one knows."

I begrudgingly agreed to see Paul that morning after breakfast. I looked through the phone book Janet kept in the drawer of the end table beside the sofa then tossed it aside when I had an idea. I ran back to my room, plugged up my laptop, connected to the first password-less Wi-Fi I could find and searched online for 'Paul's Auto Shop, Willowshire, Colorado'. Fortunately, it popped up right away.

I had the cordless phone with me ready for when I found the digits. I dialed the number, and Kate answered saying that Paul took the day off. She did, however, give me his home number to call. I nervously input the number and waited for his answer.

"Hello?" It was definitely Paul's voice.

It took me a moment, but finally, I choked out a greeting. "Hey, Paul … "

"Alexis!" His joy of hearing my voice was clear. "Is everything okay?"

• • •
82

I glanced at Salem. "Yeah; everything is fine. I just wanted to see you again ... and to say I'm sorry for the way I acted yesterday. I've done some thinking, and I want to talk about ... things ... again."

"Vampires, you mean?"

I cringed at the word. "Yeah, those."

"Okay. Do you want me to drop by your place?"

"No!" I spoke too harshly; hopefully I hadn't arisen any suspicion about Salem being here. "I'll come to you. I've been cooped up in this place by myself for way too long."

"You know, you are more than welcome to stay with me if you ever need to or want to." He sounded a little too eager.

"Thanks, I'll think about it. Where can I meet you at?" I scrawled the address down hastily and hung up. Salem watched me from the edge of my bed, anticipating what Paul and I discussed.

"I'm driving over there after breakfast, do you want anything?" I about slapped myself on the forehead. "Never mind ... "

Salem laughed. "I'll find something to satisfy my hunger while you are away."

I wasn't sure how to respond, still uncomfortable at the idea of how he fed himself. I shuddered at the thought and clambered down the stairs. I grabbed two slices of bread, popped them in the toaster and waited impatiently, and hungrily, while they cooked. Moments later, the bread jumped out of the appliance. I smeared some jam across both slices before sitting down at the dining table and eating them quickly. Salem sat across from me, watching intently. It made me feel self-conscious.

"I'll be back before too long, hopefully," I said after I finished eating, grabbed my car keys and ran outside.

I followed the directions Paul had given me. They led me into a quaint trailer park nestled between a park and an elementary school. I imagined it got quite noisy around here. I scanned through the lot, looking for trailer 16. I found it toward the very end. The trailer looked okay from the outside, if not a little unkempt—peach paneled walls, four worn steps leading up to a tiny porch. The door was flimsy; I was almost afraid that knocking on it would cause it to fall over, but I rapped my fist against it anyway.

Paul opened the door slowly, and then pulled it open completely. "Welcome to my humble abode," he said sarcastically.

"It's not so bad," I said. The entrance was cramped; to the immediate left was the living room, which could scarcely hold more than a ragged brown love seat, a TV stand and a small TV. To the right was a square dining table pressed up into the corner with only two chairs. The kitchen contained two counters, a small fridge and a microwave. Every surface seemed covered in random, indistinguishable things. I felt bad for him as I scanned the place.

"Do you want to sit down?" he asked, distracting me.

"Oh, sure," I agreed and sat on the love seat. It was surprisingly comfortable, despite the fact that I sank into the cushion.

"How are you?" he said, making an attempt at small talk.

"I'm all right ... how have you been?"

"Not bad." He smiled. "Always tired from work, but I do enjoy it."

"Work as in as a mechanic, or ... other work?" I didn't look at him as I spoke.

"Mechanic. I haven't had much 'other work' in a few months."

"That's good." I sighed, feeling uncomfortable. "I wanted to ask you something ... "

"What is it?" He sat down beside me, offering me a warm soda he grabbed from a nearby cabinet.

I popped the can open, flashing him a smile in thanks before I took a sip. It was even warmer than expected, but I drank it anyway. "I had a weird dream last night, and I was wondering if you could help me figure it out." I wracked my brain trying to figure out how I was supposed to ask Paul about this without mentioning Salem.

"Well, I ain't much of a psychiatrist or anything," he paused and chuckled, "but I'll do my best." I took pride in the fact that my vocabulary and speech varied from his—I had Desmond to thank for that one. Before he decided to leave Janet and me, he was an English teacher and actually made an effort to dedicate some of his time to helping me expand my vocabulary.

I described the dream exactly as it had happened, without naming names. Paul just stared at me intently as each word escaped my mouth. "Do you have any idea what it means?"

"Not exactly, no."

"Someone told me that your – our last name," I corrected myself, "means 'raven'. Is there any meaning behind that?"

His eyes scrutinized me carefully. "Who told you that?"

"That's not important."

"It better not be who I think it is," he replied coldly, narrowing his eyes. "But, there might be some meaning to it. Our bloodline has been around for a long, long time, and every Waldron ancestor has been involved in vampire slaying. History claims that some of them have been able to turn themselves into ravens, but it's probably just all stories and tall tales."

"Do you believe it really is just all made up?"

"Of course. I know that might sound weird coming from someone who kills the undead, but really—transforming into birds? Can you even imagine?" He shook his head, laughing lightly. "That's ridiculous."

"I guess you're right." I looked down. "There was another thing that was bothering me."

"Is it about Janet?" He frowned. I guess he must have seen the news, too.

"No. But, I am worried about her, too. I think Mark ... might have had something to do with it."

His eyes grew suspicious. "What do you mean?"

"I might have found out that he is ... he is one of them. A vampire, I mean," I whispered, worrying what Salem might think—was I betraying him by telling Paul this?

"If he is ... " he gritted his teeth as he spoke, "he'll regret having laid a hand on her."

"Calm down, Paul. I don't know that he did anything. It may have just been a bear attack like the news said."

"Either way. Have you talked to your mom?"

I told him about the conversations I had shared with Janet and about how skeptical I was of her story.

"Sounds pretty suspicious to me. Sounds like I might need to be makin' a trip to Denver."

I gulped. "Back to that other question ... " I wanted to sway him away from that conversation altogether before he did anything irrational. "What can you tell me about my mother ... my real mother?"

Paul's face displayed an expression of anguish, and I knew I wasn't going to like the story. "Her name was Destiny," he smiled faintly as he spoke her name, "we met in high school, fell in love, and got married when I was 24, she was 22. I hadn't told her my secret, I was afraid she would freak out. Of course, once I did tell her, she *did* freak out. She was very reluctant to believe who I was—what I was—but I insisted, time after time, that I wasn't crazy, and that vampires do exist. I thought she'd end up leaving me before she came 'round.

"Eventually, she had her proof, though. I took her hunting with me. She was terrified at first, but thrilled all the same. About a year later, you were born. She adored you, Alex ... " He sighed, looking at me briefly. "You look so much like her."

"I do?" I whispered, wondering exactly what my mother looked like.

"Yes, so much so it is hard to believe you are not her. You definitely have her eyes; the shape of your face is the same, your hair." He laughed lightly before his voice turned grave. "During my next hunting trip, she insisted she went along again. I tried to convince her to stay home with you, but she insisted you would be safe with a baby-sitter. She hadn't been able to go along with me in a long time due to the pregnancy and recovering and all. Well, she eventually convinced me, and I regret that I let her go more and more every day.

It was late in January; we were scouting through the woods – a common feeding ground – when one approached us. He was stronger than I had been prepared for ... I told Destiny to hide, but it was no use. I knew he could smell her; I knew he could hear her ... " He paused; I could see the grief in his eyes. "He took her from me ... from us ... I vowed that day that I would kill every last one of those bastards I could find until the day that I die.

● ● ●

That was when I sent you away. I didn't want to; you have to understand that. You were the world to me, Alex. You were all I had left of her. But it was for your own good; you were safer that way."

"I understand," I said, watching a tear trickle down his cheek. I could feel the moisture welling up in my own eyes, but I forced it back. "Paul – dad ... there is one more thing I need to know."

"Anything, Alex." He reached over and gently touched my hand. I smiled warmly, feeling closer to him than I ever had.

"What happened to the vampire that took mom?"

"He escaped," he replied bitterly. "Of all the vampires I have fought in my lifetime, he was one of the few to escape. I might not be the greatest of hunters, but it is rare that I let one get away. He was old and powerful. I can still remember the way he looks, the sound of his voice, his name." He shuddered.

"Dad ... "

"Yes?

"What was his name?"

"Raziel," he seethed, and I tried to cover up my sudden gasp at the sound of his name.

I leaned over and hugged him tightly, hoping he hadn't noticed my reaction. I wanted to hurry out of his house and find Salem to tell him what all I found out. "I am so sorry for everything you've been through. I am so sorry about mom ... "

He wrapped a bulky arm around me. "Don't worry about it, Alex." I could feel the moisture of his tears soaking through the thin material of my shirt.

"Oh, crap!" I said, releasing Paul and nearly dumping my soda on the already-stained carpet.

● ● ●

"What's the matter?" He looked alarmed and curious.

"I told a friend of mine that he could throw a party at my house tonight." I hung my head in shame. "How in the world did I get myself into this mess?!"

Paul laughed. "It's part of being a teenager."

"I've got to get home as soon as possible. Maybe I have time to talk to him and call the whole thing off."

"If high school is anything like it was when I was there, the house is probably already full!" He laughed again, with a gleam of nostalgia in his eyes.

"You're only making it worse," I grumbled. "Thanks for answering my questions."

"Anytime. Never hesitate to come over – and if the party gets out of hand, you know where to find me. I can come get you any time, and you can stay here."

"I might just take you up on that offer." I smiled and went to walk to the door.

"Oh, wait! Before you leave, I have something for you." He stood from the lumpy couch and went down the hall. I heard a door open then close, and he returned with a cardboard box. "I meant to give you this on your birthday."

"You didn't have to get me anything, Paul."

"I'm your father, of course I did." He smirked, pushing the box into my arms. "Go on, open it up."

As I pried open the box, I began wondering what he could possibly have gotten me for my birthday. I nearly dropped the box when I finally got it open: a silver and black hand crossbow lay within the core of the box. I swallowed and looked up at Paul, expecting an explanation.

"Every hunter needs a good weapon." He smiled, apparently thinking I would appreciate the gift.

I felt sick as I stared at the weapon. "I don't know what to say."

"You don't have to say anything, Alex. Let me show you how to use it," he offered, reaching over to take the bow.

"No, it's okay. I think I can figure it out," I muttered, pulling it away. "I've got to go."

"Sure, sure." He smiled again. "Maybe you will be the one that finally puts an end to that Salem Young."

It was difficult to hide my fury at his words. Salem was nothing but nice to me so far. "I have to go," I said again, grabbing the box and running out to the car. I slammed the door behind me, almost wishing it would fall off its hinges. When I got into my car, I angrily shoved the crossbow under the passenger seat.

Denver Slayings

I raced home, driving faster than I probably should have. It was midday now, which ought to give me plenty of time before the party started. When I unlocked the door and made it inside, I was relieved at all of the space around me. Paul's trailer would have made anyone claustrophobic! The scent of pizza from the previous night lingered in the air. I glanced at the living room briefly before climbing upstairs, half-expecting to find Salem. I dialed Jason's number as soon as I got in my room, but he didn't answer so I decided I would wait and call again later. I sunk down on the edge of my bed, wondering just where Salem might have gone to and when I would see him again. As strange as it was to admit, I had grown fond of his company.

An annoying light kept bouncing around the otherwise dim room, pulling me from my thoughts. I looked up and saw it was a ribbon of lights floating around on the screen of my laptop. *Just a screen saver*, I thought to myself. I wiggled the mouse to get rid of the bothersome light, and decided I might as well play around with this new toy a little while I waited to get ahold of Jason. I opened the Internet browser and typed: 'Denver, Colorado' into the search box. So many things came up that I wasn't sure what to go to. Then I saw something that made my heart sink.

"Denver Zookeeper not the only one mauled by a bear? Reports have been looming around the city of Denver, and other nearby cities, of brutal attacks similar to the attack on Zookeeper Janet Hobbs."

I clicked the link anxiously. It was a news article discussing not only the attack on Janet, but of three other people discovered in Denver with similar injuries, as well as a few in the surrounding cities.

"The only real explanation is one of the bears got loose, or there's a wild one gone mad!" says local Ms. Rachel Shetland."

"I've never seen anything like this. It's almost like the animals have gone on a rampage," says high school biology teacher and wildlife lover Leslie Woods.

"It's a coincidence. There are brutal murders and animal attacks going on all the time. There is no reason to think it's the same predator," Zoologist Mark Prince ensures.

I paused and re-read the last quote again, mostly the name of the speaker. Surely this wasn't the same Mark I thought it was. How many other Marks were there likely to be out there? A lot ... but what were the odds of it being another zoologist named Mark, in Denver? I left the news page and went back to the search engine. After scrolling down the page even further, I found something else that caught my eye.

"Colorado Slayings – Man, Bear or Mystery?"

Beneath the title, it read *"Your place for paranormal news!"*

• • •

I clicked the link curiously and was brought to a page with a black background and red text. There were links to the side relating to UFOs, crop circles, Sasquatch, Chupacabras, vampires, werewolves, witches, and all sorts of other supernatural things. I ignored them, for the time being, and spotted the article about the Denver 'slayings'. As the page loaded, I noticed I had begun shaking a little and the hairs on my arms were standing. I inhaled deeply.

"Recently, a supposed bear attack occurred at the Denver Zoo. A Ms. Janet Hobbs was viciously attacked by one of the bears while feeding the animal. Her injuries were severe, ranging from gaping scratch marks across her face and mid-section, and two identical deep puncture wounds along her right wrist. What would cause this bear to attack this woman? Not to mention, these distinct markings on her wrist do not match the bite of a bear, but more closely resemble a snake bite.

Over the past few weeks, three other Denver citizens have been found attacked—with similar injuries, namely the wrist markings. Progressively, more and more incidents were spotted in nearing cities of brutal attacks, similar to the one on Janet Hobbs (Just the most recent in this string of 'incidents') – unfortunately, most of the other victims were not as lucky as Ms. Hobbs. Is there some sadistic murderer on the loose, attacking people in the exact same manner? Is it really the fault of animals, both wild and zoo-kept? Or is this something entirely different?

Tell me—did the word 'vampire' come to mind at all as you read this article? If so, you might be on the right track. If you are familiar with my other articles, you will know that I believe these Night Walkers are lurking around in our world, preying on our blood. These are definitely no mere animal attacks.

Keep your eyes open, and be wary! They could be anywhere.
-Amanda G."

My eyes grew sore from reading the bright-red text against the black background, and my hands hadn't stopped shaking. Clearly, I wasn't the only one skeptical about these 'bear' attacks. I closed the browser and sat for a moment, thinking over what I had just read. What would Salem think, would he agree or would he think I was over-reacting and digging too deeply into this? It was odd to think how if I had found this website just a week ago I would have laughed and considered it bogus ... but not anymore.

I stepped down the stairs carefully, still a little rattled from what I had just read. The coolness of the refrigerator felt relaxing against my skin as I browsed through its core. I hadn't realized how empty it was getting—there was half a gallon of milk, some orange juice, and some leftover spaghetti from who knows when. I dumped the pasta and poured a glass of juice.

"Looks like I'll be going grocery shopping ... " I muttered aloud to myself. I searched for the envelope of funds Janet had left me with and pocketed some of the money before hiding the envelope beneath the microwave. As I was leaving the house, the phone rang, and I hastily picked it up; Karen was on the other end.

"Oh, my god, Alex! I'm so glad I got a hold of you. I've been trying to call you all morning, and you never answered! I even made a trip over to your house hoping to find you, but no one answered. I have been so worried!" She rambled on to the point that it was hard to catch each word. "I saw the news about your mom! Why didn't you tell me last night?! Are you all right? Is she okay? Do you need anything?"

Once I was positive she was done talking, I sighed and spoke into the receiver. "I'm as okay as I can be. She's in the hospital and doing better, and I'm sorry I haven't gotten hold of you. I should have known you would be panicking when you heard about it; mom was always close to you, too." I smiled at the memories of how fond Janet had been of Karen, how she often treated her like another daughter. "I've just been so overwhelmed with mom leaving and now this," I said, unable to tell her the whole truth. "And I didn't want to ruin the party you worked on for me. I'm sorry."

"I'm just glad it was nothing worse, and that you're okay."

"I'm fine, and I will let you know if I hear anything else about mom. Thanks for calling," I said awkwardly, surprised by my eagerness to get off the phone. There was so much on my mind; even a conversation with my best friend wasn't going to be enough to distract me. "I need to run to the store, and like I said—I'm so sorry."

"It's okay, Alex; I understand. Just keep in touch, okay?"

"I will," I responded and hung up.

After making a very quick grocery run, I dropped the food off at home. My attempt to get a hold of Jason failed once more. I decided to drive over to Salem's house to tell him about the site and see what he thought – assuming I could find the way there again. The twisting road was even more terrifying when I was alone, but I eased my way slowly along the asphalt. I met the familiar dirt path with a groan, not looking forward to the bumpy ride. Fortunately, the turn to the left came into view before long, and I was relieved to find I had miraculously remembered just how to get there.

● ● ●

The magnificent Victorian appeared empty when I pulled up. I sat in the parked car for a few minutes, admiring the vast house. I hadn't noticed the wide windows on the top floor before; they looked almost like two large eyes staring down at me. I shivered. My gaze was soon distracted by the surrounding nature. A cobblestone path started at the back of the house, curving off into dense foliage. My curiosity got the best of me, and I exited the car. I hoped Salem wouldn't mind me trespassing around his house.

I followed the thin, winding path through the thick forest. There were berry-speckled shrubs here and there, and the sound of rushing water. I glanced behind me, shocked that I could no longer see any evidence of the house or my car. It was amazing to be among nature for a change. A white bunny stood out from the surrounding green. I slowly approached it, wanting to get a closer look.

I jumped back and almost screamed when I saw a pale hand slowly, carefully reach through the shrubbery and grab the rabbit. It wriggled helplessly as it was pulled out of sight. The noises coming from behind the bush were unbearably disgusting—the high-pitched squeal of the poor bunny, the sickening slurping sound ... I covered my ears. I tried to run, but my legs felt like jelly. Part of me knew what was going on, but my mind wouldn't let me admit it.

"S-Salem?" I whimpered with my eyes locked on the spot where the white rabbit had stood just seconds ago.

I heard the crunch of twigs and the thump of something hitting the ground. "Alexis ... " His silky sweet voice met my ears, and I shuddered unexpectedly. "What are you doing out here?"

I couldn't see him; he was shrouded by the wilderness. "The house seemed empty, and I saw this path out here ... and I thought maybe I would go exploring while I waited for you to get back from wherever you were ... and there were no lights on ... and ... " My voice trailed off when he emerged from behind the bushes.

His appearance was startling. The light blue eyes I had begun to admire were brightly tinted with red. Blood stained his pale hands, which he promptly hid behind his back. He looked ashamed. "I was hoping to avoid you seeing me like this," he said quietly, keeping his distance.

"No ... It's okay ... " My voice was just as quiet. "I understand what you were doing, and I'm not upset."

He arched a brow. "You aren't the least bit scared?"

"Oh, no ... I'm a little disturbed." My laughter lacked any humor. "It's just something I've got to get used to, right?"

"Or you could avoid me altogether," he suggested with a frown.

"I'd rather not," I whispered.

"There is a creek not too far from here, if you would like to see it while I ... clean up."

"Sure," I replied warily, eying the spot again where the rabbit had once stood.

Twin Souls

We walked down the winding path for a few more feet until it broke off, and our shoes fell upon dark soil and gentle green moss. The sound of water grew louder with each step. As I looked around the area, I saw that we came into a clearing in the dense forest. The surrounding trees formed an arch overhead and brilliant rays of light eased through the branches and leaves. Ahead of us, beneath the archway, was a magnificent, long creek lined with large stones varying in size and color. A fallen tree lay across the water, forming a natural bridge.

I watched in awe as Salem gracefully leapt up and walked across the log. He smiled back at me expectantly, but I shook my head. There was no way I was climbing across that thing! I could easily picture myself tripping, falling into the creek and smashing my head against one of the many large creek rocks.

"I will keep you safe, you know that," he called to me as he hopped off the opposite side of the tree, ran his hands through the water and cleansed the blood off. "At least come to the water's edge."

I obliged, walking to the edge of the rippling creek. I sat on the moist soil, pulled both of my shoes and socks off, and slowly inched my feet into the shallow water. It was freezing cold!

"How can you stand how cold this is?!" I said as I pulled my feet out.

"It feels pleasant enough to me." He grinned. "Let your feet adjust to the temperature."

I reluctantly lowered my feet back into the ice-cold water. Gradually, it didn't feel quite as cold.

"See, it's not so bad."

"It's still a lot colder than I was expecting!"

Before I had a chance to react, Salem had crossed the water and was at my side, pulling me further into the water. Despite my shouts of protest, he continued dragging me in. I shivered against his chest as he held me. "It's even colder with you next to me." I laughed through chattering teeth.

He just smiled down at me. I was relieved to see his eyes had returned to their familiar pale blue. I gazed up toward the sky, noting it was beginning to darken and realized I had never gotten a chance to convince Jason not to have the party. I groaned.

"What's wrong, Alexis?" he whispered into my ear.

"It's late and I didn't get a chance to get ahold of Jason yet." I sighed.

"Oh, I see," he said, the disappointment in his voice clearly evident.

"No, not like that. Jason's just a friend. He's supposed to be throwing this big party tonight at my house, and I really don't want it. I tried to call him and have him put it off to another night or forget about it altogether, but I never got hold of him."

"Oh," he replied quietly. "Do you need to leave, then?"

"Maybe ... I don't know. Is there a phone at your place?"

"No, but that could easily be arranged." He laughed. "Or better yet ... " He held out an empty hand, and his eyes twinkled violet momentarily. A small cell phone materialized against his palm. "This ought to work."

"You're amazing, do you know that?" I grinned and took the phone from him. I quickly dialed Jason's number—finally he answered!

"Hey Jason, it's Alex," I said into the cell.

"It's about time! The party is in less than an hour, and I've been trying to call you for the past two hours!" His voice sounded a little strained.

"I tried calling you this morning, but you never picked up."

"I was out picking up some stuff for the party. Are you at home?"

"No ... " I muttered. "I'm at least twenty miles away from home."

"How am I supposed to throw this party if you're not there?!" He nearly shouted.

"There's a spare key under the owl statue beside the front walkway. I'll try to make it home before the party is over, just start without me. And remember your promise!"

"No alcohol." I could hear his voice relaxing. "You better make it; it wouldn't be the same without you."

"I'll try to make it; I promise."

"Great! So, have you tried out the laptop yet?"

A sudden queasiness overcame me as I recalled the articles I had read. "Yeah ... I used it a little today." My voice was distant. "Just to test it out. I'll definitely use it more, though."

• • •

"Awesome, glad you're using it. See you soon!" he said excitedly and hung up.

"Something is bothering you," Salem said as I hung up the phone. He took it and laid it on top of the fallen log.

"Is it that obvious?" I scowled.

"Your expressions are easy to read," he replied. "What is on your mind?"

He climbed onto the makeshift bridge and helped me up. I sat beside him, letting my feet dangle over the edge and rest in the cold water. I didn't know where to begin, whether with what I heard from Paul or what I had read online. I decided to start with the story that was less painful to tell and rambled on about the articles.

"You believe it is a vampire doing it all, then?" he asked once I finished talking.

"Yes ... I don't know. I mean, doesn't it seem a little weird to you? Before it was more about Janet than anything, but now I know the same thing has been happening to more and more people," I blurted out quickly. "How likely is it that a bear is doing all this?"

"It's not very likely at all." He grimaced. "You may have been right all along. But there is more you want to tell me."

"Yeah ... " I sighed. "This won't nearly be as easy as the stuff about the articles, though ... "

I retold the story Paul had told me early this morning, keeping my eyes focused on the rippling creek as each word fell from my mouth. Salem was silent the entire time, waiting patiently for me to finish. He cringed at the mentioning of Raziel.

"I'm so sorry, Alexis," he said quietly and draped an arm around me, pulling me closer to him.

"Would it bother you if I said I was tempted to ... help Paul find Raziel and put an end to him?"

Salem gazed down at me; I couldn't read his expression. "It doesn't bother me exactly, not in the sense you mean, anyway, but the thought of you hunting." He recoiled as he spoke the words. "Once you begin, it's hard to stop ... "

"I wouldn't hurt any more of your kind; I swear."

"You say that now. It is more the chance of you getting hurt that I do not want to think about." He shook his head. "I won't allow it. You need to avoid it at all costs. It is in your blood to be a hunter; you would not be able to stop so easily."

I didn't respond. I wasn't sure what to say. I didn't want to hurt Salem or myself, but at the same time, I hungered for vengeance against the monster who had taken my mother from me.

"There's another reason," he said, breaking the silence, and I could tell from the sound of his voice that it wasn't something I wanted to hear.

"What?"

"If you kill him, you kill me, and any other vampires he created."

"No ... " The word was barely audible. "Paul has been searching for him ever since the incident ... what if he finds him?"

"Then I can only hope he doesn't succeed." Salem frowned. "Had it not been for meeting you, I honestly wouldn't have cared to have died by now."

"Salem, what if ... " I could hardly get the words to come out, "what if Paul finds you?"

"He's found me before" He grinned slyly. "I told you already; I am smarter than he thinks. I imagine Raziel is hardly any different. In fact, he is probably smarter and quicker than I am."

"Oh ... " I wasn't sure how to respond. I sulked, leaning my head against his shoulder and thinking as I pulled my feet out of the water. "I've got one more question."

"More?" He laughed. "You are full of them!"

"I'm sorry. You would be, too, if this were the other way around!"

"I suppose you are right."

"Your accent ... it sure doesn't come from anywhere around here," I commented. "Where are you from?"

"That is one question I was actually surprised you had not asked yet. While my ancestors may have originated in Massachusetts, I was born and raised in Wales." He smiled, appearing to be reflecting on old memories.

"Wales ... " I said in awe. "How did you end up here, of all places?"

"I have traveled most of the world," he said thoughtfully. "Eventually, I decided to settle down somewhere."

"But why here?"

"You wouldn't believe me if I told you, Alexis. I know you will object because you already know my other secrets – but this is something even I cannot quite comprehend."

"I think I can handle it."

"I am not so sure." He looked up to the sky. The glow of the moon could barely be seen between the shrouds of trees. "It involves you."

I jerked my head up from his shoulder and looked directly into his pale blue eyes. "How could it have anything to do with me?"

"That is exactly why I don't think you will understand."

"Please, just tell me," I begged.

"Very well, but promise me you won't laugh."

"I promise."

"Here, take my hand," Salem said as he stood up from the log. By now, it was already dark, but I reluctantly took his hand and followed him as we began to walk further into the woods along the path. I had to know what he was going to tell me, late for the party or not.

"I am sure you have heard of Plato in school," he commented as we delved deeper into the forest.

"Yeah, sure," I said, somewhat confused. "What does that have to do with anything?"

"Let me finish," he said lightly and smiled. "According to history, he wrote of humans originally having four arms, four legs, and a single head made up of two faces." I stared awkwardly at him. "But, in fear of their power, Zeus split them all in half, condemning them to a life of searching for their other half ... I don't necessarily believe in that, however ..."

My expression told him I was still unsure where he was going with this. "Alexis, do you believe in soul mates?" I believe his cheeks would have flushed at that moment had he been human.

"I-well ... I had never really thought about it before," I replied honestly. "But, even so, why would you think I was your 'other half'?"

"Raziel, actually." He grimaced. "He said that when you bite a human, you can see their memories, and sometimes snippets of their future. He saw you ... "

"What?!" I asked incredulously.

"He didn't know you were human – especially not the daughter of a Waldron—from what I gather ... but he said he saw you and me, and in more than just the sense that we were together; we were ... *together*, a couple."

My mouth moved to speak, but nothing came out. What was I supposed to say in response to that? "You have been waiting over a hundred years for me?" I said in disbelief.

"Apparently so," he replied. "When Janet and Mark came to me, they brought a picture of you so that I would be able to identify you at school. I was awestruck when I saw it was the girl Raziel had shown me."

"That's why you're so protective of me, and why you have been so eager to be around me."

"That definitely has something to do with it." We stopped walking abruptly and Salem pulled me close to his body.

I looked up at him, "That's why you find me so 'intriguing'."

"Indeed." He smiled, his eyes lingering on my own for a mere moment before cautiously brushing his cold lips against mine. I shut my eyes and returned the gesture, wrapping my arms around him in a tight embrace. My fingers ran through his silky hair as we shared another kiss. I wanted the moment to last forever, but he suddenly pulled away. "I'm sorry," he whispered.

Why was he apologizing? I shook my head. "What for?"

"That was inappropriate," he said, averting his eyes.

I laughed. "Salem, there was nothing wrong about it. I know you come from a different time, where that might have been considered inappropriate, but really-" My words were swept away by the touch of his lips against mine again.

• • •

"I'm not sorry, then." He grinned as our lips parted once more, and he looked toward the sky. "You missed your party; I am almost certain."

My mind was void of any thoughts other than this moment until he mentioned the party. I was far too giddy at the fact that I had experienced my first kiss, even if it was not quite how I had thought it would be. I was unsure about the idea that we were somehow meant to be together, destined to meet. I wasn't quite sure how I felt about that at all, or if I truly believed it, but at this moment, I didn't care. Soul mates or not, I knew that I wanted little more than to explore this relationship with Salem. "How long have we been out here?" I wondered. Glancing at my watch, I gasped. "It's after midnight?!"

"Time flies when you are having fun they say, right?" He smiled pleasantly and leapt down from a small embankment into the water we had been sitting over earlier, the impact splashing chilling water up at me. I had been so caught up in his story that I had not realized the path had looped us back to where we started.

I shivered from the touch of the icy water, and even more so as he lifted me up from the ground and cradled me in his arms – I could feel the coldness of his skin through the material of his shirt. With how thin he was, it was difficult to believe he could so effortlessly hold my weight. I wound my arms around his neck as he carried me back to his house.

The old Victorian was invitingly warm as we entered— I half-expected Salem to put me down when we got over the threshold, but he didn't let go. I grew nervous as he smirked and carried me up the spiral staircase. I had never been to the top floor, but that wasn't what made me nervous.

"You really shouldn't be so anxious, Alexis. You know I wouldn't drop you." He playfully pretended like he was going to drop me, and I nearly shrieked.

"Don't do that!" I said, gripping ever-tighter to his body. "And you can just call me Alex, you know."

He smiled apologetically as we reached the top of the stairs. A deep red rug ran along the hallway. Framed pictures lined the walls; three of which depicted different people that I could only assume were Salem's relatives. I wanted to stop and look, but he continued walking down the hall, passed an opened door to a restroom on the left, then a closed door on the right – which I could only guess was a bedroom. Finally, we approached the last door at the end of the hall.

He pushed it open, and I was amazed by what I saw.

Seeking the Truth

The floor in the room appeared to be glass, a crystal-clear mirror reflecting everything that touched its surface. A queen-sized canopy bed sat in the center of the room draped in shining silk black sheets and blankets. Matching pillowcases covered the four pillows that rested atop the mattress. The posts holding up the bed were spiraled silver bars that held up matching silk curtains, which enclosed the bed. Two identical black nightstands sat on either side of the bed.

My eyes were fixed on the floor now, watching our reflections following us through the dim-lit room. It took me a moment to realize there was a chandelier dangling from the ceiling. Salem gently placed me on the bed, tugged the covers from beneath me and draped them across my body. The smooth silky texture felt amazing against my skin. I turned over onto my side, facing the wall and relaxing my head against the cool texture of the pillows.

"Is this your room, Salem?" I asked, shutting my eyes tiredly.

"Yes, although I don't put much use to it," he said quietly as he sat on the opposite side of the bed behind me. He ran his cold fingers through my hair and a smile spread across my lips as he asked, "Would you like to stay in the bedroom this time?"

"I already regret telling you no the first night you offered to let me stay in one of the bedrooms." I laughed lightly as I enjoyed his gentle touch.

"You are always welcome to stay here," he whispered. I could feel him closer to me now. I tensed slightly as he lay on the bed and wrapped an arm delicately around my torso. Not only was this all new to me, but there was always still that little nagging, deep down, that he could hurt me at any moment. "If you are uncomfortable, I can leave."

"No, I'm plenty comfortable," I said as I relaxed a little. "I'm just not used to any of this."

"Neither am I," he confessed.

I turned my head to look at him, "After these hundred years, you have never been with anyone like this?"

"I've been waiting for you, my twin soul," he replied quietly.

"Twin soul ... " I muttered the words sleepily. "I like that."

"Good." He smiled again and kissed me gently on the cheek. "Get some sleep. You can call to apologize to Jason tomorrow."

"Oh, no ... " I moaned, about to sit up. Salem held me down.

"There's no point in bothering him now, Alexis. He is probably asleep or at least on his way home from the party," he assured me.

"You're right." I sighed, shut my eyes and fell asleep in Salem's embrace.

* * *

When I woke up, I found Salem lying beside me, his arm still around my waist. I almost jumped up until the memory of the previous night quickly rushed back to me. Instead, I turned over and smiled happily at him. "I was certain I was dreaming again."

"Well, if you are, I hope you never wake up." He kissed me gently on the forehead. "You should call Jason after you have eaten."

"I will," I mumbled as I stretched. "What's for breakfast?"

"It's already been taken care of." He grinned. I eyed him suspiciously, noting the purple flash in his eyes. "Follow me downstairs."

Resting on the dining table was a plate of French toast triangles sprinkled with powdered sugar, a small portion of strawberries, and a glass of orange juice. Beside the plate was a glass vase with a single red rose in it. I blushed at Salem as he took my hand and led me to the table. "You shouldn't have ... " I said quietly, admiring the food hungrily.

"It isn't as if I slaved over a stove to make it." He smirked. "Hopefully you still enjoy it just the same."

"Of course I will!" I insisted and sat down. Salem sat across from me and watched me eat. I savored each bite. "Do you eat regular food?" I said after swallowing a mouthful of toast.

"No, it serves little purpose."

"Do you miss it?"

"Certainly ... " He frowned. "But at the same time it's better for my diet."

We both shared a good laugh at that, and I finished my meal. Salem then passed me the same phone I had used last night, and I redialed Jason's number. It took longer this time for him to answer.

"Hello?" Jason's groggy voice came through the cell.

"Hey Jace, how was the party?"

"It was fantastic!" he said excitedly. "It's too bad you didn't make it, though. Are you sure you are doing all right? Where were you?"

"Yeah, I'm fine," I replied casually. "I'm glad you had a good time. I just wanted to say that I was sorry for missing out on it."

"It's all right. Maybe you'll be there next time." He sounded hopeful. "I will come later to clean up; I promise."

"It's still a mess?"

"Just a little." He laughed lightly. "Don't worry about it; I'll take care of it. Now are you going to tell me where you were?"

I quickly thought up an answer. "I was out driving, and I guess I lost track of time. There's just been so much on my mind lately."

"Oh. I understand," he said. "Well, I'm just glad you're okay."

There was that phrase again – *I understand*. I knew they didn't, they couldn't. I wished I could tell Karen and him everything. "I'll be fine. Hey, listen, I need to run a few errands, but I'll talk to you later, okay?"

"Okay, have fun!"

I put the phone down and stared across the table at Salem. His mind seemed to be elsewhere at the moment and I frowned. "Salem ... " I said it quietly, part of me not wanting to disturb him. He blinked and looked at me.

"Yes?"

"I'm beyond late for school," I said as I looked down at my watch. It was after noon. Jason must have skipped school, too.

"Problem solved." He smiled, although looking somewhat ashamed. "I called in for you. You are sick with the flu, if you weren't aware."

"Oh, I am, huh?" I laughed and shook my head.

"Yes, and you are strictly on bed rest."

"I'm not entirely against that idea," I replied, reflecting on how comfortable the bed upstairs was.

"I have this nagging feeling that you are correct about the attacks in Denver," he said suddenly, extracting me from my comforting thoughts. "I thought about all you had said as I laid with you last night."

"But what can we do about it?"

"Something I would much rather avoid." He scowled, staring blankly at the dining room table. "You need to request that Paul take you to see Janet ... he will know whether Mark is the cause."

My eyes widened. "You want me to go to Denver? With Paul?"

"Either that or try to convince Paul to go on his own."

"I'll try." I stared at my half-empty plate. "Where can I throw away the rest of this?"

"Don't worry about it. I will take care of it," he said, grabbed the plate and dumped it and the remains in a trash bin that was concealed behind one of the mahogany cabinets.

"When should I try to talk to Paul?"

"Anytime-the sooner the better."

I nodded. "I guess I'll drive over to the shop."

I left Salem's house reluctantly, but promised I would return as soon as possible. The drive along the winding road was becoming more familiar and less scary. The thought of going to Denver both thrilled and terrified me. It was a sudden decision, but Salem was right—it had to be done, before it was too late.

During the drive, my mind kept going back to what Salem had told me. *Twin Souls*. I liked him, but what was I getting myself into. I had never imagined myself in a serious relationship before, let alone a destined lifelong commitment. And how could I, after all that I had seen with Janet and Desmond ... or Paul and my real mother, even? One relationship broken by lust and one by death. I wasn't sure any of the feelings I was starting to have for Salem was worth the pain I had witnessed in Janet's or Paul's eyes. Salem did seem so nice though ... so sincere in his feelings. Before I could think about the subject anymore I was approaching the auto shop, and my thoughts switched to the task at hand.

Paul was at work today, thankfully. I could see his figure moving around behind the glass windows. He was talking animatedly to a female customer. I left the Alero in the parking lot and discreetly entered the store, aiming straight for the air freshener aisle again. I listened patiently to him and the customer as I waited. Once their conversation ended, I turned around the end of the aisle and nearly bumped into my father.

"Alex!" he shouted in shock. "What a nice surprise."

"Hey," I greeted him casually. "Could we talk ... in private?"

"Of course."

The back room was identical to how it was two days prior. It felt like it had been so much longer ago. I leaned back in the familiar chair as he took his seat behind the desk again. I fidgeted anxiously as I tried to decide what to say to him.

"Is everything all right?" he asked in a caring voice.

"Yeah, I'm fine … I just need to ask you a favor."

"I'll do anything you need me to, Alex, you know that."

"Have you been keeping up to date with what's going on in Denver?"

"I have." His voice held a hint of anger. "I've been seriously thinking about taking a trip there, actually."

"That's … sort of why I came here. I think it's really important that you – or we – go and figure out what's going on over there."

"You want to go to Denver with me?" He looked stunned.

"Only if you want, or need me to."

"The more hunters the better!"

I frowned at the term. I wouldn't be there to hunt; I would be there to protect Janet and to establish a cause for these horrific deaths. "Is there anyone else that can go with us? I don't think I'd be much help if it turns out … you know."

"My sister – your aunt – Kim, she's one of us." He motioned toward a picture frame sitting on his desk. It held a photograph of him and a woman with startling green eyes and brilliant red hair.

"That's my aunt?" I asked in awe. "She is gorgeous."

He chuckled. "She'd love to meet you, Alex. I've told her so much about you."

"Well, get a hold of her as soon as possible and let's make plans to go to Denver before things get worse."

"Sounds like a plan to me … but you'll end up missing out on a few days of school."

"It's okay. I'll make up for it."

He looked unconvinced at first, but agreed. "I'll get Kim on the phone right away. Why don't you go grab a soda from the machine?"

I nodded and left the back room. The soda machine was outside in the front of the store. While I was browsing the selection, I had the feeling someone was watching me. From the corner of my eye, I could see the shape of someone standing beside me. As I put in my fifty cents, I silently hoped they were just waiting in line for the machine. The soda rolled out at the bottom of the machine, and I grabbed it, hesitating a moment before turning around.

"Oh, Kate ... it's just you," I smiled warmly.

"Hey!" The pink-haired woman grinned at me. "My shift starts in ten minutes. This is day seven of my workweek, and I am so ready for some days off."

"Seven days in a row?" I asked in shock.

"Yep. Hopefully someone else gets hired on to manage the counter soon because I'm really getting sick of all this work. I appreciate the cash, but working with no days off is going to drive me insane!"

"It would do the same to me," I said as I twisted the cap from my beverage and took a swig. I was grateful that Paul opened the door to get my attention and dragged me away from the conversation. It wasn't that I had a problem with talking to Kate, but there were more important matters at hand.

"Kim says she is ready whenever," my father said quietly as he led me back to the room. "I can set up a flight for as early as tomorrow if you're really up to it."

"The sooner the better, right?"

"Right." He smirked. "I'm so glad you are on board with this."

• • •

If only he knew I wasn't. I sighed quietly, hoping he didn't notice.

"I'll handle the flight arrangements; you head home and pack yourself a bag. You won't need much, maybe a change of clothes or two and your bathroom stuff."

"Should I meet you at the trailer tomorrow?"

"No, I'll just meet you at your house."

I frowned. This meant I wouldn't be spending the night at Salem's. "Okay, I'll be there."

Denver

Salem kept me company and helped me pack. I could tell he was nervous about me leaving, no matter how many times I assured him I would be all right. He paced around my room as I collected my bathroom items and stuffed them in my book bag.

"I could come with you," he suggested.

"Paul would recognize you in a second."

"You're right." He sighed. "I just don't feel comfortable with you being among them."

I wasn't sure whether he meant my father and aunt or the possible vampire lurking around Denver—maybe both. After my bag was fully packed we both sat on the edge of my bed, our hands intertwined.

"I'll be safe; I promise."

"Unfortunately, that is not a promise you can keep on your own," he said smugly. "Try to stay at the hospital while Paul does his ... work ... "

"That's a good idea," I replied. "I can stay with Janet. I should call to check where she's staying."

"Go ahead." He offered me the cell phone. "You should take this with you, also. I have one of my own that you can reach me at. The number is already in there." He smiled.

"Thanks." I returned the expression as I dialed Janet's number. "Hey, mom-"

"How many times do I have to tell you that she is fine?" Mark growled.

"I-I just wanted to talk to her," I said in shock "Just for a second."

"Fine, but make it quick."

"Alex?" I was relieved to hear Janet's voice. "How are you doing honey?"

"Where are you at, mom?"

"Just in a hospital here in Denver. It's not that important, really."

"Yes, it is!" I thought carefully. "I wanted to send you some flowers, but I need the address."

"Aww, that's sweet of you." I could tell she appreciated the idea. "Hang on, just a second." I heard the muffled voices again, this time Mark's voice sounded angry and loud. She whispered the address to me, and I could tell she was more than a little frightened.

"Thanks, mom ... " I mumbled. "Are you sure you don't want me to bring you home or something?"

"No, it's okay ... I'm fine where I am. Denver is my home now, sweetie." I didn't believe that for a second. "I'll talk to you later."

"Bye." I said it too late, she had already hung up.

After relaying the conversation to Salem, I heaved my bag downstairs. We were both further convinced that something was just not right. It was nearing time for Paul to arrive to pick me up, and I was growing more and more anxious as the minutes passed. Salem stayed with me, anxiously sitting on the couch beside me. He insisted he would hear the car pulling up long before they arrived.

"I wish you could go with me, Salem," I said quietly as he played with my hair.

"As do I." His voice was withdrawn, and I knew he was filled with worried thoughts still. "Please make sure to call as soon as you get to Denver. If Paul asks, tell him you are talking to Jason."

"I will," I promised.

"He will be here soon," he muttered and sat up. "Be safe, my little raven." He leaned in close and gently pressed his lips to mine before heading through the back door. I stared after him, wondering if this might be the last time I would see him.

Not two minutes later I heard the rumble of Paul's Jeep Wrangler pulling into the driveway. I stared out the back window, watching Salem vanish from sight. The knock on the front door startled me despite knowing it was about to happen, and I ran to open it. Paul stood there with a grin on his face, and beside him was the pretty red-haired woman from the photograph on his desk.

"You must be Alex," she said in a light, wispy voice. "Paul has told me so much about you."

"Sorry I can't say the same for you," I said with a frown.

"Keeping me a secret are you? Embarrassed of your little sis?" She smiled comically at Paul as she nudged him with her elbow, then looked back at me. "I can tell you everything you want to know on the trip."

"Let's get in the car; we don't want to miss our flight," Paul said, then took my bag and headed to the vehicle. "We've got a bit of a drive to even get to the airport."

The airport was packed, and it took Paul almost twenty minutes to direct us to the right side of the huge building. This was precisely why I wasn't looking forward to the trip (excluding the fact that we were possibly going to meet a hostile vampire) —airports are too busy, too crowded and too stressful. We made it through security without any issues, and made it to our terminal right on time to get in line and wait to be seated. Paul was fortunate enough to get three seats together. I wasn't sure if I felt good about that or not, but I was relieved to know I wouldn't be sitting beside some chatty stranger—plus I was interested to hear more about my aunt's life.

The seats on the plane were relatively comfortable. Aunt Kim took the window seat – apparently she had experience with sky diving and loved imagining herself soaring over the world—I took the middle and Paul was at the end. I was perfectly content until the large, rotund fellow in the seat ahead of me decided to recline his chair so far back that it crushed into my knees.

"Excuse me, sir?" Paul said politely to the man. "Could you please straighten your chair up a little; you are squishin' my daughter."

"Oh, yeah. Sure," he grumbled in response, clearly not eager to re-situate.

With great relief, I stretched out my legs and relaxed as the seat was lifted. The flight attendants gave instructions on what to do if an accident happened while in flight, and then requested everyone to put on their seat belts. I gripped onto the chair arms as the plane ascended and the flight attendant's safety instructions played through my mind—I had not braced myself for any of this. This would be my first plane ride, and I had not been anticipating the push of force against my body as we rose into the air. Kim leaned over and patted my arm reassuringly. She appeared completely at ease, almost giddy.

"You'll get used to it, trust me." She smiled. "I can't even count how many plane trips I've taken. I was nervous at first too, but now I love it."

"What do you do for a living, anyway?" I asked as I nicely declined the peanuts the attendant offered. My palms had grown sweaty as I continued to anxiously grip the arms of the chair.

"Well, outside of ... hunting ... I'm a journalist," she replied, glancing out the window. "As well as a bit of a thrill-seeker, I guess you'd say." She turned toward me and grinned. "Maybe someday I will take you skydiving."

I was certain she could see the horror in my expression. "Umm ... I think that's something I'm going to have to say no to." I laughed nervously.

"Your dad's never been too keen on the idea, either," she said, eying Paul. "It's amazing how he doesn't freak out about his side job, which is way more dangerous than parachuting out of a plane."

I laughed, trying to hide my discomfort on the subject of vampire hunting. It amazed me how open she was about discussing the subject, especially on a full plane, but no one seemed to notice. Of course, she never openly used any words beyond 'hunting', so no one would know exactly what she was talking about. If anyone did hear her, they would probably just assume she was talking about hunting animals.

"I think I'm going to try to take a nap," I said out of nowhere, despite not being tired. My mind was lost in thoughts of Salem, wondering what he was doing – probably worrying himself to death. I was also still conflicted on this sudden relationship that had been sprung on me. Sometimes the idea thrilled me, and I could feel my heart flutter, other times it was almost enough to make me queasy. I told myself it was just the flight and shut my eyes. There was so much noise on the plane that it was impossible to sleep. I could hear children crying in the back. The man in front of me was talking to the lady beside him about an authentic Italian restaurant he had gone to during a business trip to Rome. Paul and Kim were chatting across me about their plans in muffled voices. I tried to mute them out the most, not wanting to think about what was going to happen when we reached Denver. The worst of it was probably the conversation going on between the two ladies in the seats opposite ours.

"I can hardly believe so many people are flying to Denver," one of them said in a somewhat hushed tone. She had a very distinct Southern accent. "There've been so many murders here lately that you'd think no one would go. You've been seein' the news too, hadn't ya?"

"Well, Cynthia, we can't be the only ones just passin' through to Portland. You have to remember this ain't a one-stop flight. Most these people are probably headin' elsewhere and just connectin' through Denver same as us," her friend replied.

I tuned out their voices as best as I could and attempted to reflect on the other night at the creek to distract myself. I finally dozed off.

Paul shook me gently as we descended. Why, oh, why couldn't he have waited until after the matter? I was enjoying a pleasant dream that reflected memories of the night at the creek. However, that wasn't what made me unhappy about being woken up; it was the lurching of the plane as it began falling toward the ground. I was almost certain we were going to crash into the runway, but slowly the plane leveled itself. The wheels popped out, and we were safely on land again. The only thing that caused me not to feel relieved was the fact that I was going to have to endure that again on the way home.

Mark

We rented a simple little copper-colored car that Kim picked out and paid for, then headed to the address Janet had given me after Paul inserted the information into the GPS. We passed a hospital on the way, and I had an uneasy feeling we had been given the wrong address. I gasped.

"Paul ... " I mumbled as I stared at the address on the little yellow Post-it note. "I have a bad feeling."

"What is it?" he asked as he peered back from the passenger-side seat.

"I don't think Janet is in the hospital."

"What makes you think that?"

"We just passed the hospital, and that wasn't the address."

"Denver's a big place, Alex. There's bound to be a bunch of hospitals," he replied calmly. "Let's just follow the directions from the GPS and see where it takes us. Okay?"

"Okay," I said quietly, crumpling up the note in my hand. I felt around in my pocket for the cell phone Salem had given me. I browsed through the contacts and couldn't find one that said his name – probably just in case Paul got hold of it. I found Jason's number, Janet's, and Paul's among the list. My heart jumped when I saw the word 'Bat',' and I laughed out loud.

"What's so funny?" Paul asked as he looked back at me again.

"Nothing ... just a text from Jason," I lied. "I'm going to give him a call really quick, to let him know we landed safely."

"Is there somethin' going on with you two?" he said with a grin.

"No!" I said. "We're just friends!"

"Sure, sure." He laughed. "We'll be quiet so you can talk to your 'friend'."

"Thanks ... " I grumbled and set the phone to call Salem's number.

"Hello?" My stomach fluttered at the sound of his voice.

"Hey S ... Jason," I quickly corrected myself. "I just wanted to let you know we made it to Denver."

"Good. I was worried." He sounded anxious and didn't question me referring to him by Jason's name. "Where are you now?"

"We're on our way to find Janet."

"Stay at the hospital with her if you can," he insisted.

"I'm beginning to wonder if she's even at a hospital."

"Why do you say that?" The anxiousness grew.

"I'll have to tell you later, Paul's being snoopy," I muttered. "Try not to worry too much."

"You know that's impossible."

"I know."

"I miss you." There were those flutters again.

"I-I miss you, too ... " My voice trailed off when Paul glanced at me with an 'Uh huh, I knew it' look on his face. "I've got to go; we're almost at the place."

I hung up the phone and tucked it back into my pocket. The GPS alerted Kim to turn left, that our destination would then be on the right in just three hundred feet. My eyes scanned the area for a hospital, but all I saw was a row of small houses. This had to be the wrong place.

"Where's the hospital?" I said as we cruised down the street.

"You may have been right, Alex," Kim said as she stopped the car in front of one of the houses. "This is the address." She pointed out what appeared to be an abandoned house at the very end of the road.

I recalled all of the horror movies I had seen revolving around haunted houses, and this house could have been pulled directly from one of those films. Just looking at it gave me chills. The two-story building was covered in thick layers of ivy; wooden boards crossed over the two lower story windows. The windows above the awning were shattered, and I could have sworn there was a dark figure standing behind the glass, staring out at us.

"Did you see that?" I whispered to my father. I glanced back up at the window, and the figure was gone.

"I didn't see anythin'," Paul replied. I saw him lean forward in his seat and rummage through his luggage. "I'll go out first, and then you two follow behind me."

"Okay," Kim and I replied in unison.

Paul handed something over the back of his seat. I shook my head when I realized what it was—a hand-crossbow identical to the one he gave me for my birthday. "Oh, no ... I'm not taking that!" I protested. "How did you even manage to get that on a plane?!"

"It's just in case, Alex. Put it under your sweater," he instructed and ignored my question. "You have yours, Kimmy?"

"Yep, got it." She smiled.

I watched as Paul left the car and walked down the cracked sidewalk. He approached the door of the abandoned-looking house and knocked gently on the wooden door. No one responded. He turned toward us and beckoned us over. Kim and I climbed out of the car and marched along the concrete. I walked behind her, fumbling with the crossbow as I tucked it under my hoodie.

"I'm going to break down the door if no one answers this time," Paul insisted and knocked again.

"That's illegal, dad."

"See if I care," he grumbled and slammed his thick shoulder into the rickety door. It crashed loudly against the floor.

Cobwebs clung to the ceiling. The atmosphere surrounding the house gave me the creeps, but I stepped over the threshold regardless and followed them inside. There wasn't a single piece of furniture throughout the entire downstairs. The floorboards creaked noisily beneath us with each wary step. Paul turned around and held up his hand, signaling for us to stop.

"There's someone here," he whispered. I was about to ask how he knew, but then I heard a muffled voice from upstairs and something crashing into the upper floor. My dad approached the aged staircase and began climbing up it. With each step, I could picture him falling through the rotting old wood. He made it up safely then we followed quickly behind. I was beyond unprepared for this. I could feel sweat trickling down the side of my face, and my heart felt like it was about to burst through my chest. If that wasn't bad enough, the butterflies I had felt only minutes before had melted into bile in the pit of my stomach.

"You should have stayed away." I shut my eyes tightly as I heard Mark's deep voice reach my ears. I couldn't tell just where it was coming from; it seemed to reverberate off the walls.

"Where's Janet, you bastard?!" Paul shouted, holding his crossbow cautiously as he rounded the corner.

"Janet is not important," Mark hissed. "I do sense that you forgot to bring something important with you, Alexis."

I stopped behind Kim as she followed Paul into a room full of sheet-covered furniture. "I don't know what you're talking about," I replied in a croaky voice, trying my best not to lose the contents of my nervous stomach.

"I had truly hoped you would have brought Salem along with you, that way I could have killed two birds with one stone," he snickered maliciously. "Or, in this case—a bird and a 'bat', right?"

I gulped as I felt Paul's eyes turn towards me. "Salem and I have nothing to do with each other," I said bitterly, meeting my father and aunt in the room.

"Stupid kid!" Mark bellowed. "Don't think that I'm going to fall for your lies. Your father might be daft enough to believe you, but I am far wiser. I know about you and the boy."

"How? And why would you care?" I asked and ignored the angry glance Paul was directing at me.

"He is a pathetic excuse for a vampire, don't you see? Feasting on animals!" He scoffed. "He thought he could change me, too. To be 'strong' like him, but I can tell you that there is no strength in hiding in the shadows drinking animal blood. The blood of humans ... " he paused, making a deep and audible sniff with his nose. " ... is just too enticing. Too delicious. Strengthening."

"You're a monster!" I yelled, the realization that Janet had been the temptation he was talking about finally sinking in.

"A monster? Now, now ... what would Salem think if you called us such names? He and I are no different, you know? I imagine it will be little time at all before he drains you of blood, too."

"You are wrong about him. He's different!" Why had he said 'too'?

Paul was about to say something to me but Kim shook her head. "This isn't the time or place, Paul," she said.

"Just tell us where Janet is. Please!" I pleaded.

"Hurting her was a mistake; I will admit that one. At first, anyway." His voice had grown softer. "She had cut herself with a kitchen knife the morning before the ... incident ... and I tried to control myself. But once I smelled her blood, oh ... it was hard to control my thirst for more. The hunger was far too powerful."

"How many people have you hurt, Mark?" Paul spat as he spoke, turning out of the room and into the next which was roughly identical. There was only one room left, down the long hallway and at the very end.

"Oh, you know, just a few. Before Janet cut herself, I would slip away now and then and get what I could. It was never quite enough to satisfy, though." He laughed. "But all three of you should do the trick."

"So, you admit that you killed all those innocent people ... and you put Janet in the bear cage after you ... " I gasped; the rest of the words were too difficult to speak.

The wretched laugh came again, sending shivers down my spine. "And I saved the best for last."

I watched as my father inched closer to the door down the hall, steadily holding his weapon. Why had I agreed to come here? He and Kim were experienced hunters, whereas I was a coward with a shaking crossbow and feelings for a vampire. Feelings for a vampire that for all I knew could lead me to be in this same situation. What the hell was I thinking!

My thoughts of Salem vanished, and I held my breath as Paul wrapped his hand firmly around the wobbly doorknob and pushed the door open. At first, I couldn't see anything, but once my eyes adjusted I saw two red dots floating around amidst the dark void. Red, glowing eyes. The eyes of a vampire that had just eaten.

Paul tripped suddenly. I glanced downward and gasped in horror, stumbling backward.

"No! No! No!" I shouted, staring in disbelief at the body lying across the floor. Paul gathered himself and tried to ignore what he had tripped over, but I could see the anguish in his eyes.

"I simply couldn't help myself." I could see Mark's teeth shining in the darkness. I now realized what the crashing sound had been. "This is why you don't let your guard down and fall in love with a vampire."

Janet's empty, dead eyes stared up at me as I cried— this wasn't happening … it couldn't be happening! I had just spoken to her on the phone less than a day ago. The moisture behind my eyes began to cloud my vision, and the sickness in my stomach churned.

"Oh, Alex … don't cry. She begged for it after all I put her through." I could see him smirking.

"Just shoot him already, Paul!" I shrieked.

"Yes, Paul, shoot me," Mark taunted from his shroud of darkness. I realized he hadn't noticed Kim yet, and she crept noiselessly to the side of us. My father held his crossbow steadily in front of him, but he had no intent of shooting the vampire. He was the bait, the distraction, while his sister inched around the empty room.

I heard the click of her weapon. Mark flinched as the arrow seared through his skin, and yet he didn't fall over as I had anticipated – Kim had missed her target – his heart. He laughed mockingly at us. Before I had the chance to think, he was out of my line of sight. Paul and Kim turned in search of him in the darkness. My eyes grew wide as his cold hands slithered up my back and around my throat.

"Get your filthy hands off of her!" Paul said through gritted teeth.

"You might as well give up now," Mark replied, coiling his hands tightly around my neck. I gasped for air, but it was no use. I struggled, wriggling my arm between us, attempting to grasp the arrow that pierced his skin. I felt it with the tips of my fingers and put as much pressure as I could manage against it. He shrieked and pushed me away. I inhaled deeply; the rush of air burned as I consumed it. I dizzily crashed to the floor beside Janet's body.

Paul took his chance, fired an arrow, and I watched Mark stumble backwards. I let my eyes fall shut with relief, knowing that Paul hit his sad excuse for a heart. The screaming agony from the vampire lingered for only a few seconds as I fell unconscious.

Home

When I came to I was lying in an unfamiliar room, on a lumpy uncomfortable bed. The walls were covered in drab yellow wallpaper dotted with small white flowers. I groaned as I turned over on the mattress. There was a small TV set sitting on a dresser covered in flaking paint. I knew immediately that I was in a hotel, and a very cheap one at that. My neck was sore, and my mind was hazy. I leapt up as soon as my memories came back.

There was no one else present in the room, so I carefully stumbled over to the bathroom. I switched on the light and was appalled by what I saw in the small mirror over the pale yellow sink. My wavy brunette hair lay limply against my shoulders, twisted in a mess of knots. There were evident bags under my hazel eyes, and I could faintly see the light line of freckles across my cheeks. This semi-familiar girl in the mirror made me sick – especially thanks to the big black and blue marks along my throat and neck. Shuddering in disgust and anger, I discarded my clothing and headed toward the shower. I twisted the hot water on and climbed in, sitting at the bottom of the tub as the water ran down my back. I sobbed noisily as the image of Janet lying dead on the floor raced through my mind. A sudden knock on the door pulled me away from my thoughts – for which I was thankful.

"Alex? Are you okay in there?" It was Kim.

I turned the water off and draped a towel across myself. "Yeah!" I shouted as I dried off. "I'll be out in a minute!"

"Okay, just making sure," she said, and I could hear her walk away.

I pulled my clothing back on, dreading that I hadn't brought in something clean to change into. I didn't want to leave the bathroom and face them, especially Paul. I took the hotel towel and ran it along the inside of the tub, drying up as much moisture as I could before curling up inside. I pried the cell phone from my pocket and quickly dialed Salem's number.

"Alex?" His voice was just as anxious as this afternoon, if not more so.

"Salem ... " I whispered his name. "I shouldn't have come here."

"What's wrong? What happened? Are you hurt?"

"Janet's ... Janet's gone," I mumbled through a rush of sobs.

He didn't respond right away. "I'm so sorry, Alexis." I knew there wasn't much else he could say. "Are you okay?"

"Not really."

I could hear him growl; his voice had grown furious. "What did he do to you?!" he demanded.

"It's nothing ... I'll be okay," I muttered, rubbing my fingers gently across my neck. I winced at the pain.

"You are lying."

"I'll tell you ... show you ... when I get home," I mumbled.

"When are you coming home?" The anxiousness returned. "I will come get you if I have to."

"Our flight leaves in the morning."

He relaxed somewhat. "I will be waiting at your house."

"I have to go, Salem ... " I said as I heard Paul ramming his fist on the bathroom door. "I'll see you tomorrow."

Exiting the bathroom, I discovered Paul and Kim waiting expectantly for me. They both sat in dull beige armchairs beside a coffee table, each of them sipping from what were obviously beer bottles. I grimaced and sat on the bed. Both their eyes were focused intently on me.

"Are you all right?" Paul said, although I knew there was more he wanted to say.

"I guess, I mean ... no," I mumbled as I lay back on the bed. "What now?

"Now," he replied angrily, "you explain what that monster was talkin' about when he said you and Salem have been together."

"He was just trying to get under your skin ... trying to get your mind off killing him," I lied, not looking in their direction.

"Alex, I'm not the smartest man, but I know when I'm bein' lied to. Tell me the truth."

"He isn't what you think he is. He is my friend; he is the one that convinced me to see you and to come here! He is helping us!"

Paul shook his head in anger. "You *never* trust their kind!" he roared. "Your moth-Janet – trusted one and look what happened to her!"

"I'm not listening to this. You don't know him the way I do, and until you do—you have no right to say a damned thing!"

He sighed, glaring in my direction for a long time. "You weren't talkin' to Jason earlier." It was a statement, not a question.

"No, I wasn't," I confirmed.

"Give me your phone," he demanded.

"No!" I yelled. "You have no right to take anything from me."

"I'm your father."

"You've never been my father, and you never will be!"

"Alex ... "

"You have no right to take my stuff! You can't tell me what to do! 'Father' is just your title. Where were you when I was growing up and needed a father? When it was just me and Janet? Huh? I'm eighteen now—don't treat me like I'm ten!"

The look of shock and hurt on his face didn't affect me in the least. I was too angry to care – and I was right. I turned over on the mattress, facing away from them. "I'm going to bed. Don't wake me up until it's time to catch the plane," I grumbled. I was thankful that sleep enveloped me before the tears had a chance to return.

The sun shone through the thin fabric that acted as curtains, the rays fell straight across my sleeping face. I frowned as I woke up and climbed out of bed. Paul and Kim were slumped over in the armchairs, still asleep. I looked at my watch and gasped in horror. We were going to be late for the flight if we didn't leave quickly. I woke them and the three of us rushed to pack up, check out and head to the airport.

The flight home wasn't as bad as the trip to Denver, partly because I was upset to the point that I might as well have been numb. No one talked to me, and I didn't speak to them. When we landed, we walked in silence to Paul's car, and it continued as he drove me home. As we pulled into my driveway, I could see Salem's silhouette behind the windows. Something about it made me shiver, possibly from remembering the figure I saw at the house in Denver. Maybe Paul was right, should I trust Salem after seeing what Mark was capable of? After all, he had been a fellow vampire that Salem had believed was harmless. I shook my head at the thoughts, not sure what to believe.

I didn't say good-bye to Paul as I got out of the car. I slammed the door shut and raced into my house. Salem embraced me immediately, and I wondered if Paul could see us hugging through the window. I didn't care. I heard his car pull out of the driveway and felt relieved. Salem pushed me away from him slowly, looking me over, and I saw a flash of anger in his eyes as they fell upon my throat. His hands were shaking.

"Salem, it's okay," I whispered, holding his hands in an attempt to steady them.

"No, no it isn't," he growled. "Please tell me he is dead."

I nodded slowly. "Paul killed him."

"You ... " he glanced away as he spoke, "you didn't have anything to do with it, did you?"

I understood what he meant and shook my head. "No. I would have been helpless, even if I had wanted to do anything."

He pulled me into his embrace again. "I'm sorry about Janet." His voice was a mere whisper.

"Me, too ... they are having a funeral for her in a couple of days, but I don't think I can go," I said shamefully, and tried to stop the tears from starting but failed.

"That isn't something you should miss out on, regardless of how painful it might be."

"I just don't think I could take it. I don't know if I could see her ... like that." The steady stream of tears intensified, and I hoped he could still understand my broken words. "Paul and I had a fight too; I don't want to see him there either."

"What was your fight about?"

"You ... "

Salem pulled away again, his eyes looking deeply into my own. "What does he know?" He sounded almost afraid.

"Mark told him that we had been seeing each other—I don't even know how he would know that. Well ... I mean ... I guess Janet told him some, and he just figured ... I don't know. Anyway ... while we were at the hotel Paul tried to tell me I couldn't see you anymore," I replied, "I got mad, I told him he couldn't tell me what to do." I felt childish.

"We have to be very careful, Alex." He sighed heavily and led me to the couch. "I wouldn't doubt him coming after me."

"I won't let him touch you." I laid my head against him.

"I'll have better control of that than you will." He smiled gently.

My stomach growled desperately, and I realized I couldn't even remember the last time I had eaten anything. Salem seemed to catch on, and I saw his eyes flash purple. "What are you doing?" I asked curiously.

• • •

"You will see."

And I did. A bowl of strawberry ice cream appeared on the coffee table. I eyed it for a second, unsure if I really wanted it, or if I could even keep it down. Salem reached forward, grabbed it and offered me a spoonful. "It is what you eat when you are depressed, right?" He grinned, and I opened my mouth. The taste of the sweet, cold cream was amazing—possibly because it was the only thing I had eaten in almost two days. After consuming the dessert, I cuddled up against Salem and asked him what he had done while I was away, besides worry. I needed to hear something to get my mind off of Janet, to stop the tears even momentarily.

"It wasn't nearly as eventful as what you went through," he replied quietly, running his hands through my hair as I listened. "I spent most of the time here, waiting for you."

"Didn't you get bored?"

"Not at all," he mused. "I should think you would be more traumatized right now than you are."

"I don't know; I think I am just in shock. It feels like I should just wake up, and all this had been a nightmare. This is all just so unreal."

"I understand." I knew that, unlike my friends, he really did. He kissed my forehead and continued. "You have been through a lot in these last few days."

"I need a vacation." I laughed half-heartedly as I rose long enough to grab a tissue from the box nearby and wiped my nose.

"That was exactly what I was thinking," he said, and I lifted my head to look at him.

"What do you mean?"

"Let's go somewhere, away from all of these troubles."

"But Salem, I just got back from a trip ... and what about school?"

"Are you really that concerned about school?"

I thought about it for a moment, reflecting on my poor grades, my lack of interest aside from music class, and my current situation. "No," I replied honestly. "But I'm not sure if I could stand another plane trip if that was what you were thinking. And ... what about my friends?"

"We could drive," he suggested eagerly. "And your friends would always be just a phone call away."

"Salem, does this have anything to do with Paul ... ?"

"It isn't safe here anymore, for either of us."

"Why not? Your only danger is Paul, and so long as we're together I am not letting him touch you."

"I just have an uneasy feeling, Alex," he sighed. "But if you are more comfortable staying here, we just have to be extra careful."

"Let's go to your house," I suggested.

He appeared thoughtful for a moment. "As far as I know Paul doesn't know of it, so we would be safer there I suppose."

"Then, it's settled." I smiled. "We'll stay there. "

"Alex ... " His expression had been so certain, so ready, but now he looked disappointed. "I'm not sure this is the right thing to do."

"Would you rather we stayed here ... ?"

"No, it isn't that. I am stealing you away from your life."

"What life?! I just lost the only family I ever really had; my father is angry with me because I am hanging out with a vampire and my mom ... my mom is dead. What else is there?" I sounded back, angrier than I had intended.

"Wouldn't you find it strange living together so soon in our ... "

"In our what? Relationship? Look, Salem, I really like you ... you know that. And yes, I am still a little uneasy about ... about what you are, but I am a big girl. I can take care of myself, and this is what I want. I have no reason to stay in this house of memories."

He still seemed unconvinced. "Are you sure this is what you want?"

Was this what I wanted? Just hours ago I had been afraid that Mark was right, that maybe Salem could turn into a true monster. If one evening I was washing dishes in the kitchen of the Victorian and sliced my hand, would I end up drained and on the floor like Janet? Part of me didn't care either way right now. "Yes." I forced a smile and took his cold hand in mine. "Before we go, I wanted to ask you something, though."

"Another question?" He playfully groaned. "Well, let me have it."

"Mark was like you, right? He was against feeding on humans."

Salem nodded slowly.

"He said that he hadn't meant to hurt her ... that she cut herself with a knife accidentally, and the scent of her blood caused him to ... well ... do what he did." I didn't want to finish what I needed to say. "If I ... "

He put his finger to my mouth to stop me from speaking. "You have nothing to worry about, Alex." His voice was reassuring and gentle. "Mark was a young vampire, making him less capable of controlling himself in such a situation. I have much more practice."

"That sounds weird." I laughed.

"What does?" His brows rose slightly.

"The thought of him being younger than you. He looked forty, and you look my age."

"Don't go making me feel ancient, now." Salem smirked. "Let's head home."

I liked the sound of that ... maybe a little too much.

The Raven

I didn't bother packing any of my belongings—there was no sense in it when Salem could summon practically anything I desired—aside from the laptop Jason gave me for my birthday. A twinge of guilt welled up inside me as I contemplated the idea of never seeing Jason or Karen again. Then again, no one ever said I would *never* see them again. I tried my hardest to hide my struggling thoughts from Salem as we entered the old Victorian house.

"What do you want to do now?" he inquired as I set my laptop on the dining room table.

"I'm not sure," I replied honestly. "I am so used to having a schedule that tells me what I should do and where I should be and when. I'm not used to being able to just do whatever."

"Welcome to my world." He grinned. "We can do almost anything ... whatever you desire."

Just what *did* I desire? At that moment, it was a complete mystery. I knew I would have been happy just sitting on the sectional having a conversation with Salem, or reading a book in the nook beside the bookcase, but I longed

● ● ●

for something more. I pondered the idea of walking down to the creek again, but there had to be something more we could do ... something exciting enough to keep my mind off of the rest of life for a brief while. *What did I desire,* aside from the gorgeous vampire that was staring at me patiently awaiting my decision?

"The lake!" I shouted, much louder than I had intended. "I still haven't gotten to really see it yet."

Salem shrugged. "If that's what you want." He took my hand and led me behind the spiral staircase, where a door stood that led out back. We walked together along a stone path that led away from the house toward a field of bright green grass. He stared at me awkwardly for a moment as I tore off my shoes and socks. I simply grinned up at him and ran through the cool grass. It felt amazing against my bare feet. Salem stood behind, chuckling at me as I made a fool of myself.

"C'mon!" I hollered. "It feels good!"

"I'm not so sure I can appreciate it quite as much as you can."

"At least give it a try," I beckoned him over with a wide smile on my face.

Salem shook his head, still laughing, and removed his shoes. "I suppose it feels nice," he said quietly, and then grinned playfully at me.

I screamed, running toward the water's edge. I collapsed onto my back against the cool blades of grass as he pounced on me. His expression was calm and gentle.

"Did I startle you?" he asked as he rolled off of me and over to my side, staring up at the darkening sky.

"Maybe a little," I whispered, waiting for my heart to settle down. I nuzzled up against him and peered upward, following his gaze. It was strange how at peace I felt with him, despite the moments of doubt, which seemed to routinely creep into my mind. "It must be strange for you," I said thoughtfully.

"What do you mean?"

"Seeing the world change over the years."

"It has certainly been interesting," he mused. "But the world really isn't that much different. More technologically advanced, though, that's for sure."

"Doesn't it bother you?"

"No, but it doesn't much interest me either."

"What does interest you, Salem?" I asked as a shooting star soared across the darkening horizon. "Aside from me, that is."

"I have spent years reading, researching, learning to adapt to the changing world, but exploring the world was my ideal quest, until I decided to stay here."

"Am I stopping you from doing that now?" I frowned, but he couldn't see it.

"Of course you aren't," he said happily. "I have something new to experience and explore now."

I would have smiled at his comment had I not suddenly felt excessively warm, despite his cool body beside me. For some reason, the picture of Mark standing over Janet with his red eyes gleaming and that sickening smile rushed back into my mind. My palms felt clammy, and a rush of nausea overcame me. I grasped onto Salem's arm tightly, and he sat upright, lifting me up with him. I wished he hadn't—it only made me feel worse. He could tell something was wrong; I could see it in the alarmed expression on his face.

"What's wrong, Alex?" He frowned, putting his hand to my forehead. "You're burning up!"

"I-I don't know," I stuttered with panic. The world felt like it was spinning, and I clung onto him even tighter.

Salem stood, pulled me up into his arms and carried me over to the lake. "You aren't going to like this very much, but it will cool you off."

My eyes widened in fear as I realized what he was about to do. He walked into the water, and I stared downward noting with each step he took how much closer I came to touching it. "Salem, it's going to be too cold!" I cried between gasps of air.

"That's the idea," he stated and walked further in; his knees were engulfed by the darkness. Soon, his waist was hidden beneath the water's depth, and I closed my eyes tightly as I anticipated the frosty liquid touching my skin. I cringed when it first touched me, shivering against his body as he held me close. I felt little relief, however.

"It's not helping!" My eyes were still shut, and I leaned my head close against his shoulder.

"Give it time; the cold will help the fever." He didn't appear affected at all by the cold water.

I could only imagine how it appeared from his point of view: a sudden gust of wind, a whirl of black and violet feathers swarming around us. He gasped in shock, and I felt his grasp loosen. I screamed as I felt my body falling into the lake, but the cold never came. A gruesome, snapping, twisting sound came to my ears. I heard Salem's voice; he sounded frightened and concerned, but I could no longer see him. Nor could I feel him anywhere around me.

My eyes opened finally. I was hovering over the lake; I could see Salem standing several feet below me, staring up in horror. I felt lighter and at ease. Had I drowned and not realized it? Was I a spirit, suspended over my dead body as it floated down to the bottom of the lake? Maybe I had fallen asleep on the grass beside Salem, and this was all a dream. I tried to yell down to him, but no sound came.

"Alexis ... " Salem mouthed; his jaw dropped in awe. "Can you hear me?"

I failed to answer him, although I was positive I was opening my mouth. I nodded my head—maybe he would at least be able to see that.

"But you cannot speak?"

I shook my head again.

"Do you know what happened?" His eyes had yet to return to their normal size, and he looked ... scared.

My head shook once more.

"Look down ... " he murmured.

I lowered my eyes toward the now-still water, transfixed at what I saw reflected on the surface. The brunette-haired, hazel-eyed girl I was used to seeing did not stare back at me. Instead, I saw a magnificent bird with violet and blue hues shimmering against its otherwise ebony body. The wings were outstretched and flapping at its side. Piercing black, beady eyes stared back at me. The flapping ceased, and I noticed with fear that I was falling. I plummeted into the freezing water.

The sound of stretching, cracking and twisting bones came to my ears again. My eyes were wide open, but I could see nothing. I was completely surrounded by dark, cold water. Seemingly not of my own control I opened my mouth to scream and the liquid pushed itself inside, choking me. As I felt my consciousness slipping away, Salem tangled his arms under my own and pulled me to the surface.

"Alexis?" The gentle, accented voice reached my ears, but it seemed so distant. "You are safe now. You will be okay."

I struggled to open my eyes. Slowly, his face came into view. He smiled, trying to conceal his concern, worry and possibly fear. I was laying on the sectional, draped in thick wool blankets.

"Was I asleep?" My voice came out in a dull croak.

Salem shook his head. "No. You nearly drowned. Do you remember what happened?"

"I had a bizarre dream ... " I began to say, but from the look on his face, I knew something was off. "It wasn't a dream, was it?"

"No ... "

"This can't be real." I went to sit up but my head felt woozy. "Vampires were one thing, being the daughter of a vampire hunter was a whole other—but turning into a raven! This is impossible!" I shrieked. My throat burned fiercely. I curled up in a ball and covered my head with the blankets as I began coughing.

"Alex, calm down, please." Salem pulled the cover from over my head. "I mentioned to you before that it was possible ... not likely, but possible ... for Waldron's to become ravens. I at no time before imagined I would see it, and I especially never thought you would be capable ... "

"You said you thought it was a myth," I sighed, rubbing my throat.

"Legend says that only the strongest, most dangerous hunters have the ability. I admit I didn't believe any of it when Raziel first told me." He didn't look at me as he spoke. "According to him only three Waldron's had ever had the gift. You make the fourth, I suppose."

"Gift ... " I mused insincerely. "Salem, are you afraid of me?"

"No, just a little worried about what you could be capable of if Paul ever corrupted you into following his ways." He glowered.

"I have no interest in hunting, Salem!" I was hurt that he could even think I would ever harm him.

"I know, Alex," he replied, finally looking at me again. "But imagining the possibilities makes me somewhat curious."

"Curious about what?" I asked sharply, knowing where this was going.

"What you could be capable of." He turned to look away again, but I placed my hand against his cheek and held his head still. "What if you could make the world a better place ... by accepting what you are, and defeating the evil of my kind? The ones like Mark."

"You said before that it would be too dangerous." I could not believe the words coming from his mouth!

"Perhaps you could train yourself to be careful about it. Imagine if we never had to worry about creatures like him attacking innocent people, because you were there to protect them."

"You're a creature like Mark!" I reminded him bitterly.

"I am nothing like him!" he growled.

"I didn't mean it like that, Salem." I brushed my hand comfortingly across his cold cheek. "But how would I know who was the enemy and who was like you?"

He thought for a second, taking my hand from his face and lacing his fingers between mine. "You would never be alerted of their whereabouts because they would never attack anyone."

"How does Paul even know about you then? Have you hurt someone here, Salem?"

"No. Let's just say we met before, in a very uncomfortable situation," he grimaced at the memory.

"What situation?" I started to grow more and more worried that Paul had been right. What if Salem had once fed on humans? What if he ever started again?

"It was somewhat similar to the incident on the way to the creek," he muttered. I sadly recalled the white rabbit. "I was hunting late one night in a deserted park. Little did I know, this happened to be the park beside a trailer community where a vampire hunter lived. Paul was driving to the trailer when he noticed me. He knew the park was closed to civilians that late at night and stopped his car to watch me. He knew immediately what I was when he saw my eyes." He frowned. "There had been a squirrel – I cannot imagine how that makes me sound ... a vampire feasting on the blood of squirrels!"

"I would rather you drank the blood of kittens than humans."

"As would I." He smiled now. "It would seem he always had a weapon on him, just in case. He came creeping into the park, crossbow wielded and pointing directly at me. I discarded the rodent and speedily dashed behind a tree before he had a chance to shoot. I hastily told him I meant no harm, and that I wasn't like the others. He wouldn't believe me, despite the evidence lying before him. Stupidly, I even told him my name, hoping that perhaps he had heard of me in a good sense."

"At least you got away. I think he is angrier about that fact more than he is of us even being together."

"I sincerely doubt that." He laughed. "I think that is enough for tonight, Alexis. You're still weak from what happened. Come, let me put you to bed."

• • •

I woke up nestled beneath the black silk blankets of Salem's bed. To my dismay, he wasn't beside me. I stretched across the wide bed and caressed the smooth fabric with the palm of my hand. The shimmering black material felt amazing, but it sickened me all the same. It reminded me of a raven's feathers. The bedroom door creaked open slowly.

"Good morning, little raven," Salem smiled. His pet name made me squeamish when it used to make me happy. I hadn't noticed right away, but he carried a tray in his hands. I rolled my eyes, although I did appreciate the sentiment.

"And what am I having today?" I asked inquisitively as I tried, and failed, to see what lay on the tray.

I sat up, and Salem laid the tray across my lap. My mouth watered at the plate of chocolate-chip pancakes drowning in syrup, with a light dollop of whipped cream in the center. "Enjoy," he said with a pleasant smile and gently laid across the bed beside me.

I savored each sweet bite. "That was amazing!" I said as I laid my fork down and placed the tray across the top of the nightstand. My stomach didn't appreciate the meal as much as my mouth did. That feeling was lost immediately by the feeling of Salem's delicate lips against my own. I felt his tongue trace the shape of my lips, and I jumped, pulling away.

"What was that about?" I asked quietly.

"You had some syrup on your lips." He grinned playfully at first but then frowned. "I … I am sorry. I know I should not have done that, it was far too forward and early on for such things … "

I laughed and wrapped my arms around him in a tight hug. Three simple, yet powerful words fought to escape my mouth. My eyes widened at my own thoughts, and I jerked back again.

The frown on his face had returned, but before he could speak I answered his yet unspoken question. "No, it's not that. I just feel kind of sick to my stomach." It wasn't completely untrue, and it wasn't entirely from the large breakfast either.

"Oh," he said and pulled me slowly against his chest. "I'm sorry if my food made you ill."

"It's okay."

"I was thinking," he said as he ran his hand down my back in a relaxing caress. "You should see Paul again."

I gritted my teeth. "I'm not talking to him!"

"He can train you how to hunt, Alex ... if you wanted to."

My mind wasn't made up yet. It was tempting; I would admit that. But, me? A vampire hunter? It was difficult—no, impossible—to imagine. "I don't know if I want to or not."

"Paul would be pleased," he replied, speaking carefully. "You could even get on his good side again. Convince him that I upset you and you aren't seeing me anymore, he would like that. You need him, if you want to do this."

"Aren't you worried I'll get hurt?" I frowned, thinking of the possibilities. If I reacted the way I had when we encountered Mark, I was definitely in trouble. I had never been in a real fight in my life, and just holding that weapon made me nervous!

"Of course I am," his voice was soft and low, "more than you can ever know."

"Then why do you want me to do this so badly?"

"I told you already, Alex. Think of all the innocent people you could save. People like-"

"I'll think about it," I mumbled, cutting him off before he could mention Janet's name. I didn't want to lose it again.

"Your body seems prepared for you to make the decision."

I shivered. "I don't like thinking about it. How do I even control it?"

"That is something you will have to talk to Paul about, too."

"Fine." I sighed heavily. "I will talk to Paul ... but I am still really not happy with him."

Salem gave me a satisfied smile and kissed me gently. "Everything will be fine. Trust me."

And I did.

Final Farewell

After much convincing, I agreed to attend Janet's funeral. Salem offered to escort me to the event and hide out in my car until it was finished. I was anxious, distraught, and a whole mix of other emotions that I couldn't even think straight. I was hesitant to leave Salem when we drove up to the church, but he insisted I would feel better after some closure.

I wore a simple black dress and the only heels I had- which were white and clashed with the dress, but I didn't care. Who was going to notice my shoes anyway? I spotted Paul sitting in the back row of pews and pretended not to recognize him. Jason and Karen were there, too, sitting in the middle row with a few other friends of mine that had been acquainted with my mom. I waved at them briefly before scouring the funeral home for other familiar faces. I saw a few relatives that I had not seen in years, that I suppose technically were not my relatives at all. What shocked me the most was finding Desmond and Melissa sitting in the front row.

I stopped in my tracks, gazing at the dark-skinned man I had not seen in twelve years, but there was no mistaking who he was. His hair was curled and nestled against the back of his neck in a short ponytail. I scowled at his girlfriend; she didn't deserve to be here. It seemed disrespectful to bring her to the funeral of the man's ex-wife. She was perhaps in her late-twenties and had long, wavy, blonde hair that curled in fantastic loops at the ends. It took me a moment to realize Desmond was calling me over to him, and despite not wanting to, I went to him.

He draped his arms around me, which felt awkward. The last time I saw him he was much less affectionate. I felt a pang of guilt as I thought through the hateful, painful memories I had of him leaving Janet. Being a kid at the time, I could only think that he didn't love me, didn't love her, and ever since that day I couldn't find it in myself to love him anymore. Yet, had I been mistaken? He appeared so happy, so healthy, with her. Was I wrong to have hated her, too? Though if he had not left mom ... Janet ... then there wouldn't even be a funeral. I shook the thoughts from my mind as I barely returned the gesture.

"How are you faring, Alex?" Desmond asked sincerely.

I shrugged my shoulders as he released me from his arms. "I've been better."

"Understandable," he said with a frown. "You look well."

"Thanks ... so do you." It was hard to talk to him. I didn't feel like I even knew him anymore.

"Melissa and I would like to take you out to eat after this, if you would be interested," he offered casually, returning to the pew beside his girlfriend.

● ● ●

I sat a few inches away from them, eying them skeptically. "I'm not sure ... maybe," I said quietly. "I'll let you know when it's over."

The room had fallen silent as a man approached the podium before us. I had intended to listen to his words, but my mind had completely numbed as it occurred to me how real this was. The woman who had raised me, that I had known as my mother for my whole life until recently, was gone – completely – and nothing I could do or say could change that fact. The man's gentle voice faded from my ears, and I began to feel like I was watching a muted TV show, barely able to comprehend what I was seeing. Desmond tapped me on the shoulder after what had felt like mere seconds.

"Alex, hun?" he sounded concerned.

"What?" I blinked. The man was no longer up there. Everyone was lining up beside the open casket at the front of the room. I swallowed the bile that was rising in my throat. I wasn't ready for this.

"You don't look well," he commented. "You don't have to go up there, you know."

"I-I know ... " I muttered. "I don't think I can. I'm going to go get some air."

"Okay." He frowned, placing a comforting hand on my shoulder. "This isn't easy for me, either. I hope you know that."

"I know," I said, turning to leave. "I'll take you up on that offer, by the way."

His expression softened into a smile. "Great. Mel and I will meet you outside in a few."

"Okay. My car is the silver Alero; you should be able to find it," I paused, then said, "Tell mom ... tell her I love her." I started to sob uncontrollably and ran outside. I struggled to find my car through the blurring of the water in my eyes. Fumbling with the handle proved useless, but it didn't matter anymore. Salem was at my side immediately, holding me tight against his cold chest. I didn't hold back; I let the tears fall relentlessly.

His hand soothingly caressed my back, and I realized how right he was. This wasn't something I should have passed up. I may not have been able to bear seeing her, lying still and lifeless in her coffin, but I would have forever regretted not being present at the funeral at all. She may not have given birth to me, but as far as I was concerned Janet Hobbs was my mother. Salem tried to pull away from me, and I attempted to stop him, but it was useless. My strength was nothing compared to his.

"Someone is coming," he whispered and disappeared from sight.

I looked up through the haze and saw Desmond approaching; Melissa linked onto his arm. I groaned. Maybe agreeing to go out with them wasn't the brightest idea.

"I am sorry for your loss, Alex," Melissa said quietly, pulling me into her arms. "Truly." This was far more awkward than the hug I shared with Desmond.

"Thanks ... " I said, grateful that the hug didn't last long.

"Your friends – Jason and Karen – said they were sorry, too, and that they would stop by to see you later," Desmond said. Did I notice a hint of tears behind his glossy brown eyes? "I told them I would pass that along to you."

I nodded slowly. "Thanks," I repeated.

"Speaking of friends," Melissa said with a sly grin. "Who was that handsome young man comforting you just a minute ago?"

My eyes widened. She'd seen Salem. How lovely. "He's a friend," I lied. He was more than that now. In fact, despite my reservations and the little time I had known him, I was beginning to believe his soul-mate notion.

"It's too bad he ran off; we would have taken him along with us," Desmond said with a gentle smile.

"That's okay ... he'll-" My voice was broken off when I saw Salem appear from nowhere. I eyed him frantically.

"I would be happy to join you," he said, walking to my side. "I'm sorry I disappeared so suddenly, I was saying my farewells to Mrs. Hobbs."

Desmond stared at him curiously, and then smiled. "Great."

We agreed to take separate vehicles and meet up at the restaurant. It was an Italian place, which made me sicker than I anticipated. I remembered vaguely the man on the plane to Denver reminiscing about some Italian restaurant he had been to – it reminded me too much of what I had seen and endured in Denver, which had led to all of this.

We reached the restaurant shortly after Desmond and Melissa pulled into the parking lot. Salem grasped my hand tightly in his as we entered the building. The smell of fresh cooked bread was almost overwhelming. My stomach reacted immediately, growling ferociously as we followed my 'father' and his girlfriend. Our waiter led us to a table in the center of a full room. Fortunately, I didn't feel over-dressed as I scanned the surrounding tables. Women were clad in dresses, men in button-up shirts and some even tuxes. I had forgotten that Desmond could now afford to dine at these fancier places.

I scooted into my chair, Salem sitting in the one adjacent to mine. Desmond and Melissa sat on the opposite side of the table. My throat felt like it was going to swell when I noticed the shining rock on her finger. She appeared to notice my gaze and grinned.

"Don't you worry, Alex," she replied in a gentle tone. "Des and I aren't to that stage just yet."

I exhaled and smiled. "That's good to know. Well, it isn't ... that's not what I meant," I rambled and Salem gripped my hand underneath the table. The cold of his touch was somehow soothing.

"So, are you going to introduce us?" Desmond's eyes swept across the two of us.

"This is Salem," I said quietly. "I met him in music class."

"That's lovely," Melissa smiled. "Are you two, y'know ... together?"

"Something like that," Salem replied with a grin as he peeked at me through the corner of his eye.

Our waiter took our drink orders—Salem requested a glass of ice water, which I knew he would either seldom drink or not touch at all. I got a soda; Melissa followed Salem's order, and Desmond requested the finest wine they had.

"You aren't originally from around here, are you, Salem?" my foster father asked, obviously hearing the accent in his voice.

"I was born in Wales, actually," he replied with a polite smile.

"Speaking of places outside the country, where have you been off to?" I asked, eying Desmond.

He frowned somewhat, possibly hoping I hadn't noticed. "We flew in from Egypt when we heard the news," he said casually, flipping through the extravagant menu.

"Egypt is a very interesting place," Salem said, and I glanced at him fiercely. He gripped my hand tightly—

reassuringly. "My parents and I took a vacation there a few years back," he added, and I relaxed. "It's much closer to Europe than it is to America though," he added, laughing slightly.

"Are they travelers, too?" Desmond asked.

"Were," Salem corrected forlornly.

"What shall we be having this evening, ladies and gentlemen?" the waiter asked, interrupting our conversation and setting our beverages down. I took a chance to look up at him; he had tanned skin and a curved mustache above his thin lips.

Salem passed on food despite Desmond's insistence, stating he had no appetite. I wanted to say the same, but forced myself to request the lasagna. I didn't listen to the other two's orders—the dishes' names were far too complicated to understand, anyway. The waiter walked off, and I watched Salem wink at me as he took a small sip of water. I wanted to giggle, but I fought the urge.

"You two seem happy together," Desmond mused, watching us closely. "That's good."

"We are, sir," Salem said with a smile and turned to kiss me lightly on the cheek. I felt warmth rising where his mouth had touched, despite the cold of his lips.

"Good. Maybe I will have to make a trip back here in a few years for the wedding." He grinned.

I gasped as I took a sip of my soda, nearly choking. My lips moved to talk, but I couldn't make the words come out. Salem smiled back at Desmond.

"You never know," he replied, his smile ceasing to fade.

I wanted to cover my head in my hands. Fortunately, the food didn't take much longer to arrive, and our table was filled with silence as we dug into our meal. Salem simply sat and watched, sipping his ice water every now and then. I had to admit, I was glad I had opted to eat. The food was amazing! Salem and I barely spoke, just nodding and muttering the occasional "Wow's" every once in a while in a while between the stories Desmond and Melissa told us about their adventures around the globe. I could tell that Salem was somewhat eager to further discuss travel with them, but perhaps felt it would be a dangerous topic to delve too deeply into.

"How have you been, Alex?" Desmond said suddenly after recounting a long, tiring description of a trip they had taken once to New Zealand. He must have forgotten he already asked me at the funeral.

I put down my fork and looked up at him, "I've been all right, considering ... " I replied. "I know Paul is my real father now, and school is going ... not so great."

"Oh. I had no idea your moth ... Janet had told you. I must confess that is one of the reasons I brought you out to eat. That and to catch up, of course." He smiled. "And that's no good about school, Alex. You need a good education if you want to get by in this world."

"That's not always true; mom said you dropped out of school."

"There are exceptions to almost every rule, Alex. And despite being well off now I still regret dropping out to this day. I was lucky enough to get into a teaching career, despite my poor choices as a teenager."

"Well, maybe I will be lucky, too."

"Are you trying to tell me you are dropping out of school, Alex? Your mother and I raised you better than that."

Salem must have sensed the fire starting to burn under my skin and thankfully changed the conversation before I could retaliate against Desmond's remark. "Thanks

● ● ●

for taking us out, Mr. Hobbs," Salem said, feigning a yawn as Desmond finally stopped staring at me and dabbed a napkin to his lips.

"It was my pleasure. I hoped it would lighten the mood, make things a bit easier for all of us, considering."

"It was definitely good," I murmured as I chewed on a piece of bread, still angry at his comment. What kind of nerve did he have to try to say he had any true part in raising me?

The waiter returned moments later with the check, and a handful of mints. We each took one and stood up from our chairs. Desmond and Melissa walked us to the car, and I received yet another embrace and condolences from each of them. Desmond shook Salem's hand, and I wondered if he noticed how cold his skin was, but he didn't seem to react.

"Alexis, if you ever need anything … anything at all," Desmond handed me a business card with a number written messily onto the back, "you call me, okay?"

"Yeah, da … Desmond," I said as he smiled at me.

I relaxed some as I watched them wander off to their own vehicle. Salem and I climbed into the Alero and headed back to his place. All I wanted now was to curl up in bed and cry myself to sleep—I knew it was inevitable. After all the stress I had endured and emotions I had tried to hold back, it was time to let it out.

Hunting

Three weeks had passed since the funeral. Despite all that had happened, I was happier than I had ever been. Salem and I spent most of our time walking through the woods, reading one another books from his vast collection, or simply lying in the grass talking. For someone who seemed plucked from a different era, I was amazed how much we had in common. I felt as though I could spend a lifetime with him and never get bored or run out of things to say. Before long, it felt as though years had passed since I scoffed at the thought of being in a relationship with a vampire. To me, he was no longer some mythical and frightening creature. He was Salem – my charming, caring, handsome Salem. Few things could pull me from this happy existence, and one of those was ringing in my pocket.

I stopped reading the page of *Moby Dick* I was on to Salem and pulled out the familiar little cell phone. The flashing screen alerted me that it was my best friend, Karen. For a moment, I was reluctant to answer, knowing already what she would say. She and Jason had called me

• • •

innumerable times since I stopped showing up for school shortly after the funeral.

"Hello?" I said timidly.

"Alex! I swear sometimes I think you've disappeared. Are you okay?"

"I'm fine, Karen, just like last time."

"Well, excuse me for caring! So are you like, dropping out of school or what?"

"I ... I don't know."

"Well, either way I don't think you're going to be graduating with us. You've missed way too much, Alex."

"I know." She had said this all before, several times.

"I thought we were supposed to graduate together, you know? I mean we always talked about it. Walking up there in the gown, throwing the cap. What happened to that, Alex?"

"I don't know. Look, I am sorry ... really. I just don't think I can do it. I mean ... I don't think I want to."

"You know you can tell me anything, right? What's going on?"

"It's just ... mom ... and ... "

"And what? Is that boy you've been with controlling you or something? You tell me, and I will get you away from him for good!"

"No ... it's not that. Not at all. Look, I need to go. Okay? I will talk to you soon; I promise," I said, hanging up the phone.

I immediately felt guilty hanging up on Karen like that. She really was still my best friend, and I knew I should treat her better, but right now I just needed this escape. Talking to her reminded me of everything that had happened. I was much more content being hidden from reality with Salem.

Just as I had thought the disturbances from my reading were over, Salem took the opportunity to present me with yet another reoccurring pull from my happiness.

"Are you going to go to Paul's shop today?" He had been pressing the issue more and more the last few weeks.

"Fine!" I yelled, still slightly upset from the call with Karen. Despite being annoyed with him presenting this now old argument at such a bad time, he was right. I had put it off for too long. The sooner I learned to control ... whatever it was I had been 'gifted' ... the safer my remaining family and friends would be.

"I'm sorry, Salem; I was just upset. I shouldn't take it out on you. You're right ... I will go. First thing tomorrow ... "

He looked at me with suspicion for a brief moment before opening his mouth. "Good. I believe you this time. Now come on, let's finish the book. I am simply dying to know if he gets the white whale." He smiled wide.

I hit him playfully with a couch pillow. "As if you don't know, how many times have you read this? A hundred?"

"A few."

"Yeah ... a few hundred!" We both laughed for a while before resituating and continued the read.

When I arrived at Paul's shop the next morning, he was beyond shocked to see me. The surprise was soon overshadowed by his immense relief when I told him the tragic news about Salem and I 'breaking up', and that I was eager to become a hunter. More than anything, he was intrigued by the fact that I could transform into an actual raven. He had never believed it was possible, despite the legends. He was somewhat over thrilled at the fact that his daughter was one of the very few capable of such an ability. I, personally, dreaded it.

Five out of seven days of the week were spent in the back of the auto shop. Paul had it cleared out to make room for us to practice combat techniques. He taught me to use the crossbow he had gifted me. I was reluctant to begin with and my aim was very poor, but after just a week and a half, I had mastered that skill, practicing on targets he had crafted out of old emptied fuel tanks. The fact that I enjoyed the use of it scared me more than a little. Maybe Salem was right about this addiction. We practiced mostly in the late afternoon and into the night, during after-school hours because I had him believing I was still attending.

It was difficult coming up with tales to give him about how school was, what Jason and Karen were up to, and the upcoming graduation in six months. He pressured me from time to time to ask Jason out to a movie, even if Karen joined us. He wanted nothing more than for me to forget about Salem entirely. In fact, one of his main goals at training me was with the hopes that I would be the one to kill him.

We went through simple close combat techniques. At first, it was a little difficult. I had not been in a gym or done any physical activities aside from P.E. class in forever. I was actually amazed by how flexible I still was and how easily I learned to kick and punch—Janet and Desmond had put me through gymnastics and martial arts lessons as a child, but that had been so long ago. Just another group of things I had lost interest in after Desmond had abandoned us. I learned that these particular two classes had been Paul's idea, with the obvious intent of me using that skill for my future 'job'.

I was dumbfounded by how graceful Paul could be as well. I had heard from Salem how Paul wasn't the best hunter he had ever seen—how he could barely hit the broad side of a barn with his crossbow, and was far too slow to be of much concern. I was not sure if Salem had been exaggerating or if Paul had just improved ten-fold from their last encounter. Neither would have fully surprised me.

During the weeks of training, I had actually grown a lot closer to Paul than I thought imaginable. He told me that he was envious of my natural skill at fighting and my impressive aim, as well as my raven abilities. I knew he was just flattering me in some regard, but I couldn't help but to admit that I had gotten quite good. He also reflected on when he first started his training. One of his favorite memories was how he used to hunt wild game with his dad, long before he even knew of his heritage. Eventually, he began training to hunt the undead with his sister and father, but he seldom took it serious back then. He was far too focused on the relationship he had formed with Destiny, which he partially blamed for his admitted lack of skill back then. He regretted it, but at the same time was thankful that he spent so much time with her – before she was gone.

Every night after practice I went to Salem's house, exhausted and sore. Paul's plan was working, but not in the way he had hoped. With how much time I spent away practicing and in bed sleeping, I had little time with Salem. He would stay with me as I slept, and treat me to a late breakfast. That was about all the time we got together during the past three weeks.

"Are you eager to return tonight?" Salem asked, sitting across from me at the dining table. He was turning a spoon around in his fingers; the ceiling light glinted off of the metal. He appeared nervous.

"Not really." I sighed tiredly. "Paul wants me to try … changing."

"Have either of you figured out how to do that?"

"He thinks being around your kind might trigger it somehow," I said quietly. "When I am in danger, and my adrenaline is pumping … even though it didn't happen when I was around Mark."

His eyes grew cold, and the spoon clattered to the floor. "What does he expect you to do?" His voice was harsh.

"He wants to take me hunting tonight … " I murmured, barely touching the food on my plate, "real hunting, against a vampire."

Salem shut his eyes and shook his head, "No! You're not ready!"

My lips curved upward slightly. "Salem, I've had nearly a month's worth of practice. I think it's just you that isn't ready."

"You might be right." He sighed and began pacing around the room. "What if I went with you?"

"How would that work? Paul would know you were there in a second."

"I wouldn't have to be right beside you … just within the area."

"I don't know. It might work. I don't really see the point in you being there though, I'll be fine."

"If anything happened to you … " His voice trailed off.

"You'll be putting yourself in danger if you go. Don't forget about Paul."

"There is no reason to worry about me," he said assuredly.

"He's not as bad as you let on, you know."

"Do you hear yourself, Alex? This is what I was afraid of."

"I guess I'll tell Paul that I'll do it. He said I didn't have to if I wasn't ready, but I just decided that I am." I sighed, hoping I really was ready and partially ignoring

Salem's last sentiment. "He says he's been hearing some strange things down by the graveyard towards his place—people going missing and such. He thinks it may be vampire-related."

"It's possible," he said simply, though still obviously upset by what was happening.

As Salem cleared my plate, I called Paul and told him I would meet him at the graveyard. I was not looking forward to it in the least. The first experience with changing had not only been startling, but also painful. I also wasn't quite sure I was ready to face a vampire, despite all of my practice. Salem and Paul being in the same place together made me even more nervous.

The day was dragging on slowly. Salem and I snuggled up on the sofa and discussed strategies for tonight's event. He was going to leave before I did and await our arrival, concealing himself behind whatever was available, and watching to make sure I was safe. As we talked, my phone suddenly vibrated. Plucking it from my pocket, I saw Jason's name across the screen.

"It's Jason again ... " I murmured.

"Answer it," Salem suggested. "I'll leave you alone if you want."

"No, it's fine," I replied and leaned up against him again after I hit the answer button. "Hello?"

"Alex!" Jason's voice was a pleasant, welcoming sound. It felt like forever since I last heard it. As I listened, it began to sink in how much time I had spent away from my best friends. I missed a party, at my own house, because I was spending time with Salem instead. There had once been a time when Jason, Karen and I were inseparable, and now I had practically replaced them with a boy I had just met merely a month ago. Yet, despite how wretched it made me feel knowing that I had abandoned my friends, I was happier now than I had ever been before – and that just made it worse. These feelings increased at the sound of Jason's voice as he continued talking, but I did my best to suppress my emotions. "I have been so worried about you. You still haven't been to school, and I have stopped at the house countless times, and you never answer-"

"I'm fine, Jace," I said, breaking him off. I felt terrible having to sound so stern with him, but how many times where he and Karen going to tell me the same stuff?

"Right ... " He sounded sincerely worried.

"I am, honest."

"That's good." He paused for a moment before saying, "I kind of wanted to ask you something."

"What is it?" This couldn't be good.

"If you are feeling up to it ... " He paused again. "Would you want to go out for lunch, with me?"

"Um, when?" I stared at Salem hopelessly, wishing he could do or say something to save me.

"I was thinking today, but if some other time would be better ... "

The only thing that led me to agree was the hope that it would get Paul off my back. "Where'd you have in mind?"

"There's this really nice diner down by my house. Mitch works there, actually. I'm sure you know the place."

"Oh, that's cool. I guess that works."

"Great!" His voice was over-enthusiastic. "Be ready in an hour?"

"Yeah, sure."

"Are you sure you really want to go? I mean ... I've been trying to get you to hang out for like a month now, and you always say no."

"Well, you never asked me to go eat, did you?" I laughed.

"Oh, I see how it is!" he replied, laughing also. "Alright, well … I'll see you in an hour!"

"See you," I muttered and hung up the phone. Salem stared eagerly at me, awaiting my story. To my surprise, he wasn't upset.

"You need time with your friends," he insisted. "It has been far too long since you have been with them. I thought of pushing the subject other times you were on the phone but refrained."

"I don't think you understand, Salem." I sighed. "This is Jason. A boy. And he asked me out, alone."

He shrugged, "Friends can eat out alone."

"Fine," I grumbled. "I have to go home so he can pick me up."

"I'll join you," he offered.

"Okay, but don't let him see you when he shows up. I'd hate to have to make up some reason for why you are there. They still don't really know about us."

The drive away from Salem's house was frighteningly enjoyable to me now. The twists and turns no longer made me nervous. I found an unexpected thrill as we went over the hills and around the bends. Part of me didn't like this, but I tried to convince myself it was merely because I was so used to the roads. A light drizzle of rain began trickling down the windshield.

My house was freezing cold and depressingly empty when we arrived. It hurt more than I imagined, walking through the door knowing that I would never see Janet here again. I wouldn't see her anywhere again. Salem noticed my expression and pulled me into his arms. The uncontrollable tears came trickling down my face in moist, warm drops. I wiped my eyes and looked up into his eyes.

"I think I want to sell the house," I blurted out.

His eyes narrowed. "But it's your home."

"It doesn't feel like home to me anymore." I frowned. "I can stay with you."

He smiled tenderly and wiped away one of my tears. "You can stay with me without selling the place."

"There's no reason to keep it," I objected.

"It's the home you grew up in." He frowned, and I now understood why he felt so inclined to make me keep it.

"I'm sorry that your childhood home is gone, Salem ... but this house really has no meaning to me anymore ... it's just a big painful reminder. And besides, I practically live at your place already. There and Paul's."

"If that's how you feel, then I won't stop you." His expression finally softened again until he peered through the front windows.

My mouth fell open when I saw the headlights glimmering through the window, and a sudden downpour of rain reflecting in the light. I hadn't even had time to get ready! Groaning, I ran upstairs to find a pair of clean clothing, changed, then brushed my hair. It wasn't as if it really mattered, Jason had seen me in far worse conditions before. When I returned downstairs, Salem was gone. I sighed and gathered my slick red raincoat from the front closet.

Jason knocked loudly on the door, and I opened it reluctantly. To my dismay, he held a bouquet of brilliant yellow daffodils before him. His expression was cheerful but apprehensive. With a shaking hand, he offered me the flowers.

"Thanks, Jace," I said happily, hiding my discomfort.

"You're welcome." He smiled. I had never seen him nervous around me before, it was awkward. Was it just because we had not seen one another in so long? "Are you ready?"

"Yeah, just let me put these in some water." I grabbed a tall glass from one of the kitchen cabinets, ran the faucet and let it fill the cup about halfway before plopping the daffodils in it. "That should do it."

Jason led me out to his car, which was still running. He politely opened the door for me and shut it after I got in. He walked over to the other side and got situated. Once we were both buckled in, he pulled out of the driveway, and we were on our way.

The Date

The diner was smaller than I had imagined it would be. It was run by friends of the Banner family. The walls were painted a shade of deep burgundy, with lavender trim. At the entrance was a row of benches for when the place was packed. Fortunately, it was fairly empty this afternoon – possibly thanks to the sudden downpour. I recognized Mitchell standing behind the podium. He smirked at us, mostly at his older brother. His appearance was very similar to Jason's—the same shade of brunette hair, but his was curly and his eyes were blue rather than chocolate.

"Hey Jace, hey Alex," he said casually. "I'll take you to your seats."

We followed Mitchell to a cozy little booth in the back of the restaurant, right up against two large windows. The blinds were pulled up, and the brewing storm was visible. I sat down on the left side of the table; Jason took the right. Mitchell handed us each a menu and asked what we'd like to drink—we both ordered sodas, and he left to retrieve them.

"This place is nice," I commented, looking up at my childhood best friend.

"Yeah," he said and smiled. "My family comes here all the time."

"What made you decide to ask me out for lunch?" I asked curiously as I began browsing the menu.

"I have sort of wanted to ask you for a while." I looked up in shock, noting the color rising in his cheeks. "It wasn't until I ran into Paul at the supermarket that I finally got the nerve to ask. He said you could use some time out of the house."

I swore under my breath. "It doesn't surprise me that he had something to do with this," I fumed.

He frowned. "You didn't want to come?"

"No, that's not it. He's just been really bothering me lately about going out more, even though I've told him I've just been too tired."

"He's probably just worried about you."

I nodded, not wanting to talk any more on the subject. "I think I know what I want," I said.

"Great," he said. "I'll probably just get a cheeseburger. Boring, huh?"

"Probably more exciting than my grilled cheese." I chuckled. I had missed spending time with him.

Mitch returned with our drinks and asked for our orders. He winked at his brother as he left with the information. Jason's cheeks flushed again. "So, any idea what happened to that boy from music class? Karen and I haven't seen him since."

My eyes widened somewhat at his mention of Salem. "I don't know. I haven't really seen him since then either."

"Weird. Maybe he got suspended, or moves a lot or something. Or maybe he got sick." I was glad Karen had not told him whatever it was she thought she knew.

"Maybe ... " I mumbled. "How's Karen?"

"She's doing fine. She's been worried sick about you, too, though."

"Oh." I frowned and played with the wrapper from my straw. "Well, can you tell her that I'm fine? I just talked to her on the phone not that long ago … but maybe she will believe it if it comes from you."

"Of course," he answered with a grin. "Would you believe she is actually jealous that I took you out?"

I blinked and dropped the paper. "What?"

"I guess she kind of likes me." He shrugged. "I never noticed it before, we've all just been friends for so long, ya know?"

"Wow. I didn't know that either." I meant that more about him having an interest in me than Karen being interested in him. That had never been a secret to me.

"You have missed a lot of school," he commented as I took a sip of my soda. "None of it has been very exciting, though. This isn't going to screw up graduating with us is it?"

"That's not surprising." I laughed. I had forgotten what it was like talking to someone who understood what my life was like outside of vampires. "Well … "

Mitchell returned with a round tray of food at just the right time to end the conversation before it got uncomfortable. For that, I was very thankful. He placed a plate before each of us and sat a bottle of ketchup on the table.

"Thanks," I said as he walked away. I had also forgotten what it was like to have food served to me without the use of magic, and how long it takes to have a meal cooked. I could hardly imagine what it would be like to cook anything again. I laughed to myself at the thought, and Jason looked at me awkwardly.

"What's so funny?" he asked as he bit into his cheeseburger.

"Nothing," I mumbled. "I'm just happy to be here."

"Oh." He smiled wide. "Me too."

We ate in silence. So far, this was going a lot better than I had feared. Maybe Salem had been right all along and there was nothing going on outside of friendship ... but I still had my doubts.

"Hey, Alex ... " Jason's voice broke the silence suddenly, and he reached a hand across the table.

I gulped as his skin touched mine. "What?"

"Thanks a lot for coming out with me today."

"No problem." I smiled, eying his hand. "I've had fun."

"Me too." He looked away for a second. "I was kind of hoping we could do it again sometime."

"Yeah, maybe ... " I said with a frown. I was glad he wasn't looking directly at me.

"I was kind of thinking maybe next week we could see a movie, maybe ... If you're up for it?"

"We'll see," I replied, not wanting to hurt his feelings.

"Do you have other plans or something?"

"No ... not exactly. If something comes up, I'll let you know."

"Okay." He smiled again. Mitchell returned, gave him the check and walked off. "There's something else I wanted to talk about."

"What is it?" I asked reluctantly.

"My parents ... " He sighed, barely able to speak the words. "My parents are getting a divorce."

"What?! How did that happen? They've always seemed so happy!"

"Exactly. They've *seemed* happy. But they haven't been. It was dad's idea, he said there is no more passion in their marriage, and he doesn't want to go on if things are going to stay that way," he explained. "I'm thinking of looking for a place to move to. I can hardly stand the arguing and fighting anymore. With the money I get at Howard's, I should be able to afford something small."

I frowned. "I'm so sorry, Jason. I had no idea."

"Yeah, me either really," he said, smiling just slightly. "It will be okay, though. Do you want me to take you home after this?"

"Sure," I mumbled, deep in thought about Mr. and Mrs. Banner. They had always been such a cheerful, happy couple. It was bizarre thinking it had all been a facade.

Jason let go of my hand long enough to pay for the meal and get out of his seat. As soon as we were standing, he reached over casually and took it again and didn't let go again until we reached the car. He once again opened the door for me before getting in on his side.

"Alex," he said calmly, buckling himself in and glanced at me. "I had a nice time, really."

"Yeah, it was fun," I said, looking back at him. That was my first mistake. I was shocked at how close he was to my face. "Jason-" before I got the rest of my words out, his lips were against mine. I pushed him away, possibly a little harder than I had intended and his opposite shoulder slammed against the car door. All of the training with Paul had made me stronger than I realized.

"I'm sorry," he mumbled, rubbing his shoulder. "I shouldn't have done that. I don't know what I was thinking."

"It's okay ... " I said quietly, averting my eyes. "I just ... I just wasn't expecting it, is all."

"You liked it, then?" His voice was hopeful.

I couldn't answer him. "Let's just wait before we do that again," I murmured. "Just take me home, please."

"Okay ... " He sounded upset, but I tried to ignore the urge to comfort him. "I'm sorry. I hope you aren't mad at me. I just ... "

"I'm just ... surprised, that's all. Let's just go. Please."

After a short, silent drive, we reached my house. I said bye quickly and ran inside. Salem was waiting patiently on the sofa, reading a book. I hesitated for a moment, then walked into the room and greeted him. He could tell that I was upset.

"What happened?" he asked as he set the book aside. "Did you not have a nice time?"

"I did up until the end," I grumbled and slumped down on the couch. "Jason kissed me."

Salem stared at me, a flicker of anger illuminating his eyes with a hint of crimson. I had never seen him react in such a way; it was startling. He clenched his fists tightly. "Salem ... " I whispered as I backed away slightly, "Your eyes ... "

"Did you ... " He didn't finish the sentence as he ignored me. He sighed and looked away from me. "Did you return it?"

"No!" I shouted. "I can't believe you would even ask that!"

"I just wouldn't be completely surprised if you saw something better about him." His lips were set in a firm, straight line. "The warmth, the lack of worrying about Paul, living a normal life again ... "

I shook my head in anger. "You obviously don't know me as well as I thought!" I got up to leave the room, but the cold fingers lacing around my arm stopped me.

"Don't leave, Alex," he whispered in a gentle voice. "I apologize for my behavior ... "

• • •

"You're the one that said I should go. You're the one that said-"

"You're right." He sighed, turning me around to face him. His expression was more relaxed, and his eyes were natural again. "I'm not used to having competition."

"You don't have any competition. He's my best friend, who clearly thinks I want to be more than that ... and I think I have Paul to thank for that later."

Salem didn't reply, instead he put his arms around me, dipped me downward slightly and kissed me deeply. My head was spinning, but I wasn't complaining—it was a good feeling this time. He pulled me up and kissed me again, this time more gently. "I want my lips to be the only ones to ever touch yours," he whispered in my ear.

"Salem ... " I replied quietly, pressing my body against his. Those three words came to mind again, and I pushed them away. "Salem ... why were your eyes red when I told you that?"

"Anger can cause that to happen." He frowned. "Unfortunately, it's not something easily controlled."

"Oh ... " I said as I thought it over. "I should get ready for tonight."

He regrettably loosened me from his embrace, and I sauntered upstairs to shower. I got dressed in an entirely black outfit—Paul insisted it would be easier to sneak around the cemetery if I blended in with the darkness. I could hear a car pulling into the driveway as I wandered downstairs. I wasn't ready yet ... then again, would I ever be?

"Salem?" I said as I entered the kitchen. I sighed sadly, realizing he said he would leave before Paul, and I did. I wondered if I would even notice him when I got there—part of me hoped I wouldn't, and I truly hoped Paul didn't find him.

• • •

When I went to open the door, I peered through the window and noticed with shock that the rain had turned to snow. Gentle flakes were whirling through the air, illuminated by the lights on Paul's Wrangler—so much for blending in with the surroundings. I grabbed my crossbow from one of the kitchen drawers and headed out to the car.

The drive to the cemetery was tense. I avoided eye contact with Paul as I furiously thought over what happened between Jason and me. I decided to wait until a later time to bring it up. There were far more important things I had to focus on – like getting a grip on my nerves. Paul pulled the car over about a mile away from the cemetery to make it less conspicuous. We walked the rest of the way in silence; my jaw tightly clenched as I fought the urge to yell at him about Jason.

The graveyard was surprisingly beautiful and depressing at the same time. A light dusting of snow covered the ground, sprinkled across the tops of the tombstones and the realistic silk flowers lain before them. There were sparse trees spread throughout the cemetery, their brown leaves holding on loosely and seemingly as dead as the corpses in the ground. I wondered where Salem might be hiding, but I tried to avoid searching for him. A sudden crunching sound reached my ear, and I turned to look at Paul – from the look on his face, I knew he had heard it, too.

"Be very quiet," he whispered in a tone so low that it was hardly audible. "Someone's here."

I nodded my head, following slowly behind him as he crept toward a large crypt in the very back of the cemetery. I noticed we were surrounded by a tall wrought-iron fence from all sides other than the small gate we had entered through. I hoped I could run fast enough to reach the gate, or else climb over the fence, if necessary.

● ● ●

Someone whimpered from behind the crypt. My heart leapt in my chest, thumping loud and hard as we approached the tomb. Then, a voice came – it was a woman speaking in a comforting voice.

"It won't hurt long, precious," she said soothingly. "Just relax."

"P-please ... " The new voice was young and gentle, but terrified.

Paul glanced back at me and signaled for me to go around the other side. I nodded and stepped to the right of the building as he inched to the left. My weapon was out; my hands were steady, and I was ready for whatever hid behind that building—or so I thought.

The image before me made me gasp in horror. A little girl, maybe eight years old, curled up on the ground beneath a tall woman with a mess of black hair falling in strands from her scalp. Salem was right—he was an exception. This woman may have once been beautiful, but her face was distorted and hideous from the hunger in her eyes. I gulped at the sight of the two long fangs easing out below her upper lip. She turned away from her prey; her eyes now focused on me.

"More snacksss," she hissed. "What a pleasant surprise!"

Paul came from behind the crypt, tugged the girl away and faded from view. I was left alone to face this monster. She leapt into the air – I was amazed by how high she could jump! I spun around, looking for her. She was behind me now, preparing to pounce. I swung my weapon in her direction, pulled the trigger and released an arrow. It punctured her throat, and a line of thick blood oozed out. My eyes grew wide as I felt the familiar nausea and discomfort from the night at the lake.

● ● ●

"No, no, no ... " I muttered to myself. Although I knew this was part of Paul's plan, I didn't want it to happen. I shrieked in agony as my bones twisted and snapped, shrinking and curling into the shape of the raven. I was soaring above the vampire within seconds, my wings flapping beside me at ease. How is a raven supposed to defeat a vampire? I wondered to myself.

"Open your mouth, Alex!" I heard Paul shouting to me, but I didn't see him.

What use was that going to be? I opened my mouth—or beak, rather—and a loud caw reverberated off the surrounding tombstones. The vampire clutched her hands to the side of her head as if she were in agony. "They can't stand the sound!" Paul yelled.

I flew down, cawing once more as I landed on the vampire's shoulders. She tried to bat me away, but I wouldn't budge. Without much thought, I pierced her skin with my beak, and she screamed, flailing her arms before crashing to the snow-covered ground. I flitted my wings behind me and jumped off of her body. My eyes, although perhaps not the ones visible to the outside world, were wide with fear and confusion. Her body writhed and wriggled on the snow, as if I had severely damaged her.

The snapping, crunching sound came again. I flinched as a burst of radiant feathers surrounded me, and I fell upon the frosty ground beside her. She took the chance to clamber to her feet, although she was still in evident pain. Suddenly, she was on top of me. My hands grasped onto her shoulders, and I pushed her away with all the might I could muster, shoving her into a nearby tombstone. I caught sight of my crossbow lying idly in the snow, and I crawled over to it, aimed it in her direction and shot again. She moved before it could hit her. Something had clearly weakened her, but it hadn't been enough.

Before I had time to react, her body was over mine again. Her long, thick nails clawed at my skin as I tried to hold her back. I screeched as the nails dug deep into my shoulders. The monster of a woman cackled, and then opened her mouth wide. Salem had been right; I was not only going to get hurt out here – I was going to die.

Something moved outside my line of sight, and my heart sunk when I realized it wasn't who I had expected. Salem, with glowing red eyes, appeared beside us. He swiftly kicked the female vampire as hard as he could in her ribs, knocking her off of my body. He tackled her to the ground, and I stared in fear as his fangs were bared.

"No, Salem!" I shouted, but he didn't listen. His teeth tore deep into her flesh, and I shut my eyes.

Paul finally came into view, the sound of his boots crunching in the newly fallen snow made me open my eyes. He stood a few feet away, wielding his crossbow and preparing to shoot either one of them. I panicked, ran into him and pushed him over as the trigger went off. My mouth fell open, and I expected a howl of agony to erupt, but no sound came. I rolled over onto the snow, grasping at the shaft in my side.

Paul's lips trembled as he stared at the arrow embedded in my skin.

I fought to keep my eyes open, fought to focus on where Salem was, but everything was spinning so fast and growing hazy. "Salem ... " I gasped, and I was swallowed by darkness.

Poison

"Get away from her, Paul!" Salem said fiercely. I could feel something wet and cold beneath me as I suddenly regained a bit of consciousness and realized I was still lying in the snow. My eyes were open, but I could hardly focus. My father knelt beside me, his eyes frantically staring from my face to the wound in my side.

"I'm not leaving her, you monster!" Paul replied through gritted teeth. "If I wasn't so worried about her, I would kill you right now!"

"Do you not realize that I saved her life?!" Salem shouted.

"That doesn't make you any better than the rest of them."

I could hear my own shallow breathing and the faint sound of painful moans. "Salem … " I coughed.

"She wants me, Paul," he said in anguish. "I can help her, *please.*"

Through the haze, I could see my father stand and back away. Salem was at my side now; his cold hand gently brushed against the side of my face. "Alexis? Can you hear me?"

I nodded my head weakly and shivered. "Salem ... is she ... "

"She's dead," he assured me. "Try not to move."

I wasn't sure at first why he wanted me to remain still until I felt his hand at the base of the arrow. "No!" I cried out in pain.

"It has to come out," he said calmly.

My body shook with unbearable pain as he tore the arrow from my skin in one swift motion. The screams I heard didn't sound like my own—they sounded horrific and terrifying. I curled up in the snow, holding my arms tightly against myself trying to stop the shaking. Salem gathered me into his arms and held me.

"It's okay, Alex," he whispered soothingly. "The pain will fade soon; I promise. Thankfully, it didn't hit any organs, just tissue."

"What happened ... to the little girl?" I gasped as I remembered the vampire's poor victim. From the look on Salem's face, I knew I didn't want the answer.

Paul stared at us angrily. "How did you know she would be here?!" he demanded, ignoring my question entirely.

"That's really not important right now, Paul," Salem seethed.

"Don't forget I could kill you where you stand, monster."

"P-please, stop fighting," I pleaded, shivering against his cold body.

"Let me take her somewhere warm," Salem said, lifting me up as he stood.

"No. I can take her to a hospital," Paul objected.

• • •

"It burns!" I screamed. "Salem ... it burns!" I squirmed violently in his arms.

He stared at me with confusion, and then turned his frightened gaze toward my father. "Please tell me those were just normal arrows."

Paul frowned and shook his head.

"What is on them?!" Salem demanded, cradling me in his arms.

"They're tipped with venom," he said in shame. "It helps weaken your kind for when we miss our mark."

"Is it fatal, Paul?" Salem's voice was pleading now.

Paul didn't answer.

"Is it?!" Salem shouted.

"I honestly don't know," he muttered. "I've never shot a human before."

"You better pray it isn't," Salem growled and began running at speeds faster than I had ever imagined possible.

I could vaguely feel the smooth silk beneath me, and see a figure pacing back and forth at the front of the room. Everything looked like it was shrouded in a mist of fog, and my head ached as if I had been bludgeoned with a bat. I groaned and pulled my hands to my face.

"Alex?" Salem's sweet voice reached my ears. Where was he?

"S-Salem ... " I whispered between a sudden shiver.

"Are you cold?" He sounded absolutely devastated.

"N-no. I'm okay. Where are you?" I felt around the bed for him, and then the realization washed over me; he was the figure pacing at the end of the bed. I felt his weight hit the mattress as he lay beside me. His cold hand met my clammy forehead.

"You're running a fever," he said sadly. "Do you remember anything from last night?"

I wracked my brain in an attempt to recall the previous night. Images flashed through my mind of myself floating over a blurred figure, Salem pouncing through the darkness, and Paul was there, too. I shook my head; this didn't make sense. They wouldn't have been together; dad would have killed Salem.

"Why were you and Paul together last night?" I mumbled groggily.

He relayed the memory, and it all came to me in sudden images. "No ... " I groaned. "Paul saw you!"

"That's not important right now, Alex," he said quietly, pulling me against him. "How do you feel?"

"Confused." I laughed bitterly. "A little sore, too ... and everything is blurry."

"It will fade," he whispered comfortingly into my ear, his embrace tightening. "Are you hungry?"

"No," I said and laid my head against his chest. "What do we do now?"

"Nothing has changed, Alex."

"Paul knows."

"He doesn't necessarily know anything. For all he knows, I am stalking your every move."

I laughed. "Did that noise bother you?" I mumbled, somewhat embarrassed. Why should I be?

"A little." He grimaced. "I wasn't aware a raven could be so powerful. Like I said, I have only heard stories."

I sighed contentedly as I relaxed against him. "How did I hurt her so badly? That's what I really don't understand. It was just a peck, really."

"I think it's similar to the arrows," he spoke quietly, hesitantly – not wanting to upset me, I suspected. "Perhaps

Waldron ravens are capable of producing venom that is harmful to my kind."

I shook my head. "None of this makes any sense Salem. Ravens are just birds. Birds don't have poison."

"Listen to what you are saying, Alex," he sad and chuckled. "You are lying against a vampire, and you spontaneously turn into a bird! How is the idea of being capable of such damage outside of reason, knowing this?"

"Because ... we're just birds!" I shouted. I wasn't sure why I was acting like this, maybe it was just the confusion still swirling around in my head from the night before.

"You aren't a mere bird! You are far more than that. It is scarcely different from me being able to do this." His eyes flickered purple and a bowl of chicken noodle soup appeared on my nightstand. "I've been through this with you before; the world isn't at all how you may have once believed. Waldron's have always been strong and dangerous to my kind, and clearly, they have developed a form of poison that weakens us," he explained with slight distaste. "Now, get some food in you. It will make you feel better."

I wanted to reject the soup, but I knew he was right. I began feeling better after I consumed just half the bowl, and I could feel my fever starting to pass. Salem said the fluids probably helped dilute the poison in my system. He disposed of my half-devoured meal and returned immediately.

"How do you feel now?" he inquired, brushing a strand of hair from my face. "You're no longer clammy; that's a good sign." He smiled pleasantly.

I shuddered as he flashed his teeth at me. An image of him with deadly fangs entered my mind, and I wondered unwillingly how exactly he had killed the female vampire. "I'm okay ... " I muttered, lost in thought.

"You seem frightened." He frowned and sat beside me again.

"I just … have a lot on my mind, about last night. I saw you attack her."

He glanced away temporarily. "I'm sorry you had to see that."

"Don't apologize. It was just sort of unexpected, and scary," I said honestly. "I never thought you could be like that."

He laughed quietly. "I can do plenty of frightening things, Alexis. The important thing is that I don't, unless necessary … such as last night."

I nodded mutely as I considered this. "I don't think I want to practice hunting anymore."

"If that's how you feel, I won't pressure you to continue, but I think it might be wise of you to reconsider."

"Why?! For what purpose! I nearly got myself killed last night!"

He cringed at my words. "That was of no fault of your own. Paul is more to blame for that than anyone else. You did exceptionally well."

I shook my head and sighed. "I just don't know if I can handle it."

"Don't change your mind just yet, Alex." He pulled me close again. "What you are doing is a good thing, and I will always make sure you are safe."

"I guess." I sighed in defeat.
He smiled and kissed me lightly on the forehead. "You'll have plenty of time to think once you have rested."

● ● ●

The Woods

A mere week had passed before I was out on the battlefield again. Despite my initial reservations, I had decided that this was what I wanted. This time I would fight solo. My feud with Paul was not over, and I hadn't spoken to him since the incident, despite his constant phone calls. I stalked through the cemetery again—my father was right about it being a common feeding ground. I found my target leaning against the base of one of the many tall trees. He eyed me hungrily; a devious smirk painted across his pale face. His skin was rugged and dirty, and his build was tall and muscular.

"Fancy meeting you here," he said casually, flipping a golden coin in his left hand.

I eyed him curiously. "Were you expecting me?"

"Word has been going around that there's a raven among these parts," he replied smugly. "I just had to come and see what all the fuss was about. I never imagined it would be a little girl."

Where could he possibly have caught word of that? My eyes didn't leave his. I had anticipated a scene similar to my prior visit to the graveyard, but instead it appeared that I was the victim. I reached for my crossbow, but he was much too quick. The coin flipped one last time, landing with a quiet *clink* against the top of a nearby gravestone. His cold hands were suddenly wrapped around my wrist, preventing me from grabbing my weapon.

"You will be the first raven I have tasted." He grinned maliciously, leaning his face toward my throat.

"You won't be tasting anything tonight I'm afraid," I replied calmly. With my available arm, I punched him hard in the jaw. He fell back, stunned by my strength, but within seconds his laughter resumed.

"A feisty one, I see," he remarked. "You are just making this more enjoyable for me. I haven't had a challenge in a long time, and despite what my dear mother always told me – I don't mind playing with my food."

"I'm glad you are having so much fun right before you die," I replied fiercely. He sprung at me, but I rolled out of the way. My head slammed into a rock behind me. I was hardly aware of the damage at first. The man's nostrils flared as the scent of my blood reached his nose, and he licked his pale, thick lips hungrily. My fingers found the spot on the back of my head; I could feel moisture against my fingertips.

The distraction was enough for him to get the opportunity he had anticipated. I staggered to get up, but he lunged toward me with full force. The stone behind me crumbled beneath our combined weight. I could feel the rough rock stabbing into my back as I laid there helpless for a moment. His mouth opened wide, revealing his stained yellow fangs. I shuddered and tried to block out the memory of Salem, but it was impossible.

• • •

"You are truly making this too easy for me, raven! And here I thought I had a real fight on my hands for once," he snarled, his lips nearing my throat once more.

"You got lucky." I kneed him as hard as I could between the legs, sending him hurtling over my head and behind me. Grabbing my crossbow, I turned and pointed it toward his chest.

"Considering the rumors I have heard of your family's shooting skill, that's not going to do you much good," he barked with laughter.

"Unfortunately for you, I have better aim." I pulled the trigger. The arrow whistled through the air, and the vampire, caught up in his own banter, was too slow to realize what was happening. I grimaced as he fell to the ground, a bloodcurdling scream emitting from his gaping mouth. My eyes were wide with horror as I watched the vampire's body contort in misery. Despite what he was, I couldn't control the pain I felt at watching him die.

Salem appeared at my side from some place unseen. He wrapped his arms around my waist and pulled me away from the horrific scene. "I was afraid for a moment," he whispered. "I almost intervened."

"How does it not affect you like it does the rest of them?" I asked, "The blood; I mean."

"There is a difference between human and animal blood," he commented after checking my scalp—the damage wasn't severe. We walked away from the dying vampire. "Over time I have not only grown accustom to animal blood, but I enjoy it. Your blood actually smells—and probably tastes—quite revolting to me now."

"Thanks," I said sarcastically, not quite sure if that was a compliment or not.

"You were quite impressive out there." He smiled, although it was obviously forced.

"Do I scare you?" I asked in wonder.

"You don't, but what you are capable of certainly does. I am very fortunate to know you will never turn against me like that" He paused and looked at me. "You won't, will you?"

"Of course not!"

"Good." This time his smile was sincere. "I was thinking tomorrow, perhaps we would go back to the creek."

"That would be nice," I said as we walked to my car. "Will you be eating innocent bunnies again?"

He glared at me momentarily, and then shrugged. "Possibly. I should, actually."

"You don't eat as nearly as much as I would imagine," I spoke quietly, opening my door and getting in.

When he was inside, he looked at me. "I don't enjoy it the same way they do. Let me try to put it in a perspective you might understand. Food is intended as fuel, but humans are weak and easily give in to temptation, ignoring that fact. They will eat and eat, no matter how full they might be, simply because they enjoy the taste. That's similar to how a vampire feeds ... they will go beyond what is necessary to keep them going, because they thirst for more. I may have grown fond for the taste of animal blood, but I only drink what I need."

As I thought this over, Mark's wretched voice came to mind *"Once I smelled her blood, oh ... it was hard to control my thirst for more! The hunger was far too powerful."* I felt sick to my stomach thinking about it, about Janet.

"That makes sense," I mumbled as we drove to the old Victorian. "I've done some thinking, Salem ... and I sort of want your opinion."

"On what?" There was an edge to his voice.

"My house," I replied simply. "Now, before you say anything—I'm not going to sell it."

He smiled at that. "Good."

"I want to rent it out. I was thinking I could offer it for cheap to Jason." I noticed the unsettling look on Salem's face and placed my hand against his. "His parents are going through a divorce. It would be good for him, and I think it'd be good for me, too. I don't want to stay there anymore, especially when I could just stay at yours."

There was a hint of a smile in the corners of his mouth. "Are you asking to move in with me?"

"I might as well be already, right?"

"Considering you spend every night there, yes." The sound of his laughter was pleasing to my ears. "If that's what you want to do, I won't stop you. Giving it to Jason leaves you the opportunity to visit the house whenever. And you will still own it, of course."

"Right."

His expression changed suddenly when we pulled into the driveway. He climbed out of the vehicle, despite it still moving, and raced toward the front door. I noticed in horror that the stained-glass windows were shattered. Shards of green and blue sparkled under the porch light.

I deserted the car and followed Salem into the house. There was no evidence of theft, but someone had definitely broken in. I felt sick as I glanced around the living room, noting that the only things that had been touched were my belongings, which led me to one conclusion.

"I think I know who did this," I said angrily.

"Paul," Salem snarled furiously. "His scent is lingering in the air."

"This is bad, Salem ... this is bad ... " I mumbled as I realized what this meant.

"We should just be thankful we were away," he said, calming down some. "But I don't doubt he will return. I will keep a vigilant watch for him, Alex ... and if he tries anything, I cannot promise I won't hurt him."

"I-I understand," I stuttered, watching him gather a broom from the front closet and sweep up the mess of glass from the porch. "Do you want me to do that?" I offered as I ignored the haunting possibility of Salem killing my father, or vice versa.

"No, it's fine," he answered with a smile. "But thank you."

"What are you going to do about the windows?" I frowned. "They were so beautiful."

"Do you really need to ask?" He laughed gently.

"Oh, right. Magic," I replied. He dumped the shattered glass into the garbage and glanced at me curiously.

"Does it bother you?"

"No, but I want to try something. I want to make my own meal tonight."

"Why? You don't like mine." He put on a fake pout.

"Don't be silly," I replied with a chuckle. "It's just something I'd like to do, because I sort of miss it."

"I understand," he said. "Go ahead. But, I will provide the ingredients."

"Deal."

I told him each ingredient I wanted for my dinner. As I opened the mahogany cabinets, I watched in amazement as a box of Rotini noodles appeared with a jar of pasta sauce directly next to it. I glanced back at him and grinned. "Thanks," I said and began prepping my pasta. The water boiled slowly on the black stove top, and my stomach was not in the mood to be patient. I was beginning to rethink my request to not have my food magically prepared.

"I had forgotten how long this can take!" I said miserably as bubbles slowly began to rise in the pot.

"Someone is quite impatient," Salem said playfully behind me. He was sitting at the dining room table, studying the empty holes on the front door.

"What's on your mind?" I asked as I dumped a small portion of noodles into the pot.

"Simply wondering what they should look like this time."

"You don't want them to look the same as before?" I stirred the noodles slowly to prevent them from sticking.

He shook his head. "No. I have something else in mind."

"Really? What?"

"I'm afraid you will have to wait and see." He grinned at me.

"Okay, fine." I laughed, eager to see what it was. A question suddenly popped into my head, and I stopped stirring abruptly. "How do you think Paul found this place?"

"He could have followed us at some point. That's the only logical explanation I can come up with."

When my pasta was done, I sat across from him at the table and began eating. I no longer felt self-conscious when he watched me eat. Plus, his attention was apparently someplace else tonight as he gazed thoughtfully at the door. After eating, I spent the next two hours curled up in the nook chair reading through portions of the book he had made for me. Before I knew it, I had dozed off. The book slipped from my fingers and crashed noisily on the ground.

I jumped up and gasped at the sound, then sighed with relief when I acknowledged the cause. My vision was fuzzy at first, but once it adjusted I realized Salem was nowhere to be seen. I half-expected him to be on the sofa, or even at the dining table. I picked up the book and laid it on one of the shelves beside the chair. As I stumbled tiredly into the kitchen, my gaze was immediately drawn to the front door.

The windows had been replaced by slick new ones. The backdrop was made up of misshapen colorful stained glass varying in blues, greens, and purples. Against the left window was the image in the shape of an ebony bat. Beside the bat, on the opposite window, was the image of a raven painted in a mixture of black, blue and purple. I had to step back to realize the creature's wings were curved into the shape of the upper half of a heart, while their bottom halves were connected at the tail to form the end of the heart.

The scream that burst through my lips sounded powerful enough to shatter the new windows when Salem came up from behind and twisted his arms around my waist.

"You scared me!" I gasped, relaxing into his embrace.

"I noticed," he said and chuckled lightly. "What do you think of it?"

"It's beautiful," I said, admiring the windows still. "It does make me want to ask though ... "

"No, vampires can't turn into bats, as I have told you already," he spoke as though he had read my mind. "It was the only thing I could think of that made sense."

"I like it," I said happily. "A lot!"

"I'm glad." He turned me around to face him. "You didn't sleep very long."

"You're right." I knew what was coming. I couldn't fight the exhaustion forever.

I kissed him gently once, and he took my hand, leading me upstairs. There was a light on in the hallway, illuminating the picture frames along the walls. I stopped abruptly behind Salem and gazed at the images. The first one to catch my eyes was the photograph of a little girl cradled in a woman's arms. They both had brilliant blonde hair that reminded me of spun gold. The woman was wearing a simple white gown with blue trim along the neckline and a wide happy smile across her lips. The child was bundled up in a wool blanket with her head nestled against the woman's bosom. I took my eyes off of the picture to look at Salem; his eyes were withdrawn and sorrowful.

"This is Hannah and your mother, isn't it?" I asked in a gentle, yet curious voice.

"Yes." His answer was simple, and I could tell it hurt him to even look at the pictures, which made me wonder why he even had them.

"Did you 'make' these?" I asked, knowing it was impossible for such pictures to have existed back when his family was alive – not to mention they would have burned in the fire.

"Of course ... my memories of their faces are so vivid; it's almost painful." He frowned. I squeezed his hand gently.

"They were beautiful, Salem." I smiled despite his sadness. "What was your mother's name?"

"Margaret," he said fondly, "everyone called her Maggie, though. And my father's name was Arthur." He directed my attention to a gold-framed picture slightly higher up on the wall. The image depicted a fine young man with similar features to Salem's, notably the black hair. Arthur's hair was pulled back in a ponytail, and he had a faint mustache above his upper lip. He wore thin spectacles that made him appear slightly older than he was.

"I was starting to wonder where you got your hair from," I said as I looked up at him. "You definitely have Maggie's eyes, though."

"Personally, I am grateful I didn't inherit her hair." He smiled, and then pointed up at another picture, set in between the other two. It was of a beautiful boy—perhaps ten-years-old—sitting in a rocking chair holding a black kitten on his lap. I knew without a doubt who I was looking at.

"You were handsome even then," I said in awe.

"Oh, you mean to say you weren't ogling at the cat?" He grinned as I playfully slapped him on the arm.

"No, I wasn't, although he is cute, too." I shook my head, smiling. "Did the cat have a name?"

"He didn't have a name for a long time, actually," he mused. "We generally referred to him simply as 'Kitty', until Hannah was old enough to speak. They had an amazing bond." He smiled sadly. "She named him Daniel."

My brows furrowed. "That's a weird name for a cat."

Salem shrugged. "When my mother inquired about the source of the name, she said it was the name of a man she met ... but Hannah was obviously too young to know anyone, so my parents assumed she had created an imaginary friend and passed the name along to the cat."

"Wow," I whispered. "And what's behind this other door?" I asked, indicating the mysterious door on the right wall, beside the picture frames.

"That's the guest bedroom." He shrugged again. "It was empty before you arrived ... I had intended for you to use it the first night you stayed, but considering you objected that offer ... "

"How do you remember them so vividly, Salem?" I asked suddenly, remembering how he had once told me that his memory of his mortal life was vague.

"I suppose those were some of the memories I didn't repress."

• • •

Before I had the chance to say anymore, Salem had me in his arms and was carrying me off to bed.

127

The air outside was chilly, and the sky showed promise of snow. Salem and I walked hand-in-hand toward the clearing. I could tell from the thoughtful expression pasted on his face that he was up to something, but I kept quiet. I wore a thick sweater over a long-sleeved shirt, but shivered nevertheless. Salem, however, was completely at ease wearing a pale blue short-sleeved T-shirt that made his eyes appear even brighter than usual. I envied him at that moment. In fact, I envied many things about him. Immortality, while he spoke of it as a curse, was something any human ought to lust for. Never having to sleep! I could only imagine the possibilities. How many books could I consume in the saved time I would have from not sleeping— or how well I could learn to play the piano!

I was pulled from my thoughts when Salem spoke, announcing our arrival. We were a few feet away from the creek, which was covered with a thin sheet of ice. I shivered just from the sight of it.

• • •

"Are you sure this was a good idea?" I laughed. "I would hate to actually get the flu, although Karma probably owes it to me."

"Don't worry." He smiled. That familiar violet glimmer in his eyes appeared, and I knew something was about to happen. "Close your eyes," he whispered.

I obeyed, awaiting his command to reopen them.

"Go ahead, open them."

My nose reacted before my eyes had the chance. I could smell the distinct aroma of burning wood. Then my ears recognized the sound of crackling embers. I opened my eyes to find a bright, billowing fire amongst a pile of logs that hadn't previously been there. Lying roughly three feet from the warm fire was a lavender blanket laid out across the grass. Atop the blanket was an unopened basket. I eyed Salem curiously. "What's this all about?" I asked.

"I'll tell you in a moment," he said with a sly smile. He sat down on the blanket and patted the empty space beside him.

I sat next to him, and he opened the basket to reveal a sliver of cake identical to the one I had asked for the first night we met. "Well, this can't be in celebration of the day we met," I said as I tried to piece everything together.

"No, you are right. It isn't." He offered me a fork. "November 12th, 1885 was my birthday."

My eyes widened as I realized what he was saying. "Today would be your birthday!" I gasped. "Why didn't you tell me?"

"It actually sort of slipped my mind." He shrugged. "It's not something I really think about anymore."

I reached over and hugged him tightly. "Happy birthday Salem!" I kissed him delicately on the cheek. "I can't even imagine how nice it must be not to have to actually get older on your birthday."

His eyes were dark. "Alex ... do you remember what I said to you the first day we met? About being blessed with another year of life on your birthday?"

"Of course." I nodded, taking a bite of the cake. "Why?"

"Today might be my birthday, but it truly isn't something to celebrate." How had this gone from a celebration to a moment of sadness? "While you get to continue growing, aging ... I'm stuck like this."

"I think of it the exact opposite," I said thoughtfully, putting my fork down. "Aging isn't fun—it's scary. Knowing that someday I will be fragile, wrinkled, old, and eventually die ... " I shuddered at the idea. "You, on the other hand, you will be the same for the rest of time."

He stared at me for a long time without speaking. I allowed him to have his moment of silence while I indulged in more cake. "I suppose I understand it from your point of view," he said quietly.

"Good," I replied. "It's much more depressing on my side of things, I think. You still get to live, even if you don't age. What's so special about aging, anyway?"

His eyes were now focusing on the fire, and I wondered if it was bothering him with memories of his family's death. "It's most every human's dream to go through the natural course of life. You're a child; you go to school; you learn; you finish school; you meet someone special, you get married; you have a family; you grow old together, and you die together." The orange hues of the fire danced in the darkness of his pupils. "That opportunity was stripped from me."

"Not completely ... " I put my fork down again, no longer interested in eating. "Salem, you have seen so much more than any human ever could. You have spent years traveling, reading, learning. We get a limited time on this planet, while you get all the time in the world!" He turned his gaze on me again "Plus, you don't need to be human to meet someone special, right?"

His expression softened. "Of course not" He pushed the basket and cake away and pulled me to him. "Let's not spend this whole afternoon dwelling on that," he said with a smile and pressed his lips gently to mine.

I went to return the kiss when he jerked away suddenly, his eyes alert and scanning the area. "What-" He pushed a finger to my lips before I could finish speaking. Then, I heard it, too: a faint rustling nearby. I breathed a sigh of relief when I noticed it was just a doe galloping through the clearing. Salem's lips twitched slightly.

"Do you mind ... if I ... " His words trailed off. "Stay here, for a moment. I'll be right back."

I nodded, knowing what he was doing. I covered my ears, awaiting the sound of the poor animal losing its life. I watched the fire weave back and forth as the wind pushed against it, and a shudder ran through me. Salem returned moments later, a hint of red in his eyes, but I tried to ignore it. He sat beside me again.

"Where were we?" I smiled, leaning in to kiss him again. He was hesitant at first, then pulled me down onto the blanket and kissed me deeply. My hands traced down the side of his face, across his neck, then rested against his collarbone. Our lips parted slowly and I inhaled deeply, the cold air rushing through my lungs.

I kissed him once more before laying my head against his chest. My hand fell across his heart, where it rested for a few moments and I tilted my head up to look at him.

"It's weird," I said quietly, "not being able to hear your heart beat … because, it doesn't … "

His face was expressionless. "Yours beats enough for the both of us."

I noticed then how erratic my heart was beating. I blushed. "I'm sorry."

"Don't be," he said tenderly. "It's among my favorite sounds."

Our peaceful, comfortable, picnic was interrupted again as an extra chilly wind pushed across us, making the blanket flap and bunch up. Salem lifted me off of him and sat me up, this time his eyes were startled. "Alex, we need to leave." His voice was urgent.

"What? Why?"

"Paul is here, somewhere," he hissed.

"You saw him?" I asked anxiously, glancing around.

"I smelled him, on the wind." He took the beautiful blanket and patted down the fire with it, putting out the flames. "We have to go, *now*!"

A twig crunched. Salem growled and spun around. It was too late. Paul stood across the clearing, peering at us from behind a tree. His face displayed a look of utter disgust. I wondered how long he had been watching, and what all he had seen or heard. My heart was racing even more now.

"Alex!" Paul roared at me. "Get away from him!"

"No!" I shouted. "You shouldn't be here!"

"Neither should you," he replied through gritted teeth. "Do you want to end up like Janet?"

● ● ●

"Don't you ever use her name against me. Salem isn't Mark! I have every reason to be here," I argued. "You've done more harm to me than he ever has … to anyone!"

I could tell my words struck him hard, but he shook his head. "Give me one good reason why I shouldn't just kill him right now, Alexis!" Paul shouted fiercely, aiming his crossbow in Salem's direction.

Out here in the clearing, with the radiant sunlight directly on his face, Salem's pale skin was more defined. The light, purple lines beneath his eyes were evident—in fact, I wasn't sure I had ever noticed them before now. He stood between my father and me, as if protecting *me* from Paul.

"You can't kill him, because … because I love him!" I shrieked from the top of my lungs.

"Damn it, Alex! Why'd you have to get into this mess?!" Paul yelled furiously.

Salem dropped his gaze from my father and turned swiftly to face me. I knew this was a mistake by the mischievous grin forming on my father's face.

My lips quivered; my stomach grew queasy. "Salem, move!"

It was too late. Everything happened so quickly, too quickly: the click of the crossbow firing, Salem turning abruptly to face Paul, the sharp arrow soaring through the sky, Salem's agonizing scream as he crumbled to the ground. I stared in horror at him lying in the soft grass. I fell to my knees, screaming profanities at Paul, telling him to leave, telling him I hated him. He gave me one last glance—a look of betrayal marking his ashen face—before he ran from the clearing. I crawled over to Salem's still body. The tears began falling, and I didn't make any effort to stop them.

"Salem … oh, Salem, please … " I sobbed, pressing my hand against his cold cheek. "Please … "

He smiled weakly. "Alex, it's okay ... " he whispered hoarsely. "Look away, for a second ... "

I nodded my head slowly, relief pulsing through me as I turned my head. When he moaned in pain again I had to fight the longing to look, to make sure he was okay. Something snapped, and this time I couldn't help but look. Betwixt his fingers was two halves of the arrow. My eyes fell immediately on the hole in his chest, directly below his heart. "He missed," I whispered.

Salem smiled gently through the pain, "Typical for him ... fortunately."

"The poison isn't causing you any discomfort?"

"Not enough to do anything permanent, I don't think. I just ... just feel a little weak."

I watched the wound steadily heal until there was scarce evidence that he had been injured at all. He sat up slowly, flinching as if he were still in immense pain, and then wrapped his arms around me. "Say it again," he spoke quietly, his lips right at my ear.

"I love you, Salem ... " I said, my heart thumping in my chest.

I could feel his lips form into a smile. "I love you, too," he said tenderly and held me tightly within his embrace.

"Salem, why didn't you run from Paul or something ... instead of turning toward him?" My eyes were confused, if not a little irritated by how close to death he had brought himself.

"I knew he would miss," he answered assuredly. "He always does. That man has some poor aim for a hunter."

"You didn't *know* he would! He seemed to hit his mark more often than not in training. How many times has he come after you?"

Salem laughed. "This is may be the fourth time. I told you, hunters underestimate me, or in his case— overestimates himself. You've got to remember that training is not the same as the real thing. You should know that as well as anyone, after what happened your first night.

"You have to promise me something, Alex," he said suddenly. "If you for any reason speak to Paul, or anyone who knows him as a hunter, I need you to pretend like he did succeed ... "

"You want me to pretend you are dead?"

"Yes. That way, he won't be after me anymore at all."

"Okay," I promised. "You should've just moved away from here the first time he came after you," I said with a sigh.

"I had my reasons not to." He smiled and kissed below my ear.

"What reasons?" I asked, although I knew the answer.

"*You.*"

School

The following morning I was not surprised to find the ground covered in a fresh blanket of snow. It glimmered against the faint sunlight that peeked through a canopy of clouds. Salem was downstairs when I awoke, curled up comfortably on the sectional indulging in a book. He immediately jumped up from the couch and wrapped his arms around me.

"Good morning." I laughed happily as I returned the hug. "How long has the snow been coming down?"

"At least three hours," he answered. "Breakfast is waiting for you in the kitchen. I hope you don't mind."

"Of course not," I said as I unwound myself from his arms and waltzed into the kitchen. "What is this?" I asked as I stared at the misshapen, slightly-burnt pancakes on my plate.

He shrugged and sat down. "I attempted to make you something from scratch, since you were so eager to not have your food magically prepared ... "

I shook my head and laughed. "I said I wanted to cook because I missed doing it. I don't have anything against you summoning my meals. I especially prefer it over burnt pancakes."

"It was at least interesting for me," he said with a chuckle. "I don't mind if you don't want to eat it, I wouldn't if I were you," he said with a look of disgust. "I can't even remember the last time I cooked anything, if I ever have for that matter."

"Well, it's been far too long." I laughed again and dumped the food into the garbage. "Now, summon me something delicious!" I grinned.

A plate of fresh, steaming waffles covered in strawberries appeared on the table. It definitely looked more appetizing than what he had cooked. "Thank you," I said and began eating. "What's the plan for today?"

"You have some voice mails from Paul," he said without glancing up. "I listened to them. I hope that is okay."

"Of course," I said as I swallowed a mouthful of strawberry. "So, what does he want?"

"He's received a lot of phone calls relating to your absence from school ... I guess he was your next contact listed after your foster mother."

"Oh." I grimaced then shrugged. "I'm old enough that I can just drop out. In fact, I'll do it later today."

He frowned at my response. "I don't want you to do that."

"Too bad," I replied stubbornly. "It's way too late for me to catch up on everything this year anyway. If I didn't drop I would have to go again. The only thing I had been looking forward to was graduating with Jason and Karen, but it is too late for that. What else did he have to say?"

"There were several furious messages filled with profanities, about how disappointed he is, how hurt he is, and repulsed." he frowned. "I am truly messing up your life."

"No, you're making it better, trust me. It isn't your fault that Paul can't accept you for what you are."

"He also said that Jason was in an accident." His voice was low and careful as he spoke, watching for my reaction.

"What?!" I leapt up from my seat, nearly knocking my plate onto the floor. "What happened? Is he okay?"

"Calm down. He's fine; he just suffered a broken arm and a few gashes. Paul didn't say much relating to the incident, so you might want to call Jason."

"Why didn't you tell me as soon as you found out?!"

I didn't hesitate for a moment; I didn't care to even hear his answer. I ran up to the bedroom, grabbed my cell phone and input Jason's number. Waiting for him to answer felt like forever, but finally, I heard his voice.

"Hello?" He sounded hoarse and tired.

"Jason! Are you okay? Paul left me a message saying you were hurt." I wondered if he could understand me through my rushed words.

He laughed. "I'm all right; it's nothing too serious. My arm is in a cast, and I had to get a few stitches on my shoulder."

I sighed with relief. "What happened?"

"I was driving home from Howard's last night and hit a slick spot on the road. My car slid and another car slammed into the side of me." His voice changed abruptly—a hint of remorse.

"Was the other driver okay?" I asked hesitantly.

"He was fine ... " He sighed. "But his wife didn't make it."

"Oh, no!" I gasped. "That's awful!"

"Yeah," he mumbled. "I can't help but feel like it's my fault somehow, even though it was nothing either of us could control."

"Don't let it get to you, Jace," I said reassuringly. "Would you be able to meet me somewhere? I kind of need to talk to you about something important."

"Of course!" The enthusiasm in his voice was evident; it was nice to know that I had a friend still eager to see me. "Where'd you have in mind? It has to be somewhere within walking distance ... my car's in the shop."

"My house," I replied. "Are you sure you are okay to walk? I can just pick you up if you want."

"No, it's fine; I think I can manage. The pain medicine has done the trick." He laughed. "When do you want me to come by?

"An hour or so?"

"Okay, I'll start getting ready as soon as we hang up!" He laughed again.

"Sounds like a plan. I'll see you there."

I quickly told Salem what had happened and where I was going. He offered to join me, obviously uncomfortable with me being alone with Jason again, but I insisted it wouldn't be safe—Jason could tell Paul. First, I made a quick stop at the high school and did exactly as I told Salem I would—I went to pull myself out of school completely, hoping I wouldn't regret it at some later date. For now, there was no point in me being enrolled in school. There were far greater things that I could devote my time to—like saving my hometown from the undead.

It felt like a long time had passed as I sat in the school parking lot contemplating what I was about to do. Was I making the right decision? Would I later regret it? I almost backed out before finally mustering up the courage and headed for the school doors.

It was odd being among the familiar surroundings of my school. I could plainly see my locker as I walked down the hall toward the principal's office. Memories ran through my mind of Jason, Karen and me laughing together while we walked down the halls, something that I hoped I would never forget or miss too much. My pace slowed as I neared the office, my heart beginning to pound as I pushed the door open.

The office aid eyed me curiously, and then smiled warmly at my presence. I wasn't very familiar with the woman, but she appeared gentle and friendly. She wore her dirty blonde hair up in a messy bun, and a thin layer of makeup concealed her true self. I approached the desk and requested to speak to the principal.

"May I ask your name, please?" she said in a sweet, polite tone.

"Alexis Hobbs," I replied, tempted to say Waldron as I was growing used to the name.

"Are you over your flu, Ms. Hobbs?"

"What? Oh, yeah." I felt my cheeks grow warm. "Thanks for asking."

The office aid smiled and dialed the number to the principal to check to see if he was preoccupied. "You are welcome to go in, Ms. Hobbs," she said after hanging up the phone.

I nodded and slowly crossed over to the beige door in the corner of the small lobby. My nerves were overwhelming and I nearly backed out again, but I knew this was something I wanted to do. I pushed open the door and found myself face-to-face with Principal Norbert.

"Excuse me, Ms. Hobbs," he said bashfully and stepped back. "Caroline hadn't warned me that she told you to come in; I was about to come get you."

"That's okay." I laughed uncomfortably and followed him into the room. He sat behind the desk, and I sat on the opposite side in an uncomfortable blue chair.

"What might I help you with?"

"I came to drop out of school," I said a little too quietly, but he appeared to hear me clearly.

He leaned forward on his desk, clasping his fingers together and staring at me quizzically. "Are you positive that is something you want to do, Ms. Hobbs? You are already through 90 percent of public school, why stop so close to the end? You need your diploma. How will you afford a home without a diploma?"

"I already have a house."

"You cannot expect to be given everything in life. This is more important than you might realize, Ms. Hobbs. Isn't there something you desire to do with your life after high school?"

I couldn't very well tell him the true reason why I was dropping out of school, but my mind was at a loss for excuses. "I can get an ordinary job at minimum wage if I have to."

The principal scowled and shook his head. "You show so much promise in music class, from what Mr. Collins has mentioned in the teacher's lounge. You don't want to continue on to a music career? There are college courses on the science of music, you know?"

I shrugged. "It's not that important to me," I lied. "It's just a hobby."

"Have you thought about how this will impact others? What of your future family. Children are expensive, Ms. Hobbs. A minimum-wage job will not cover that. And what about much later in life? Have you thought about retirement? Working a minimum-wage job until you are sixty or seventy and then having to scrape by off of a few hundred dollars a month from social security is not a pleasant life. My mother did just that, and I would not wish it on anyone."

I had never even thought about the notion of ever having children, and for the briefest moment, I wondered if vampires could have children. "She seemed to raise a successful enough kid," I replied firmly.

He attempted to persuade me even more for the next fifteen minutes, but I didn't have time to listen anymore. By now, Jason was probably at my house waiting for me, and was no doubt freezing, stuck outside in the cold. I gave Principal Norbert my final decision and despite his ill attempts to convince me otherwise, my drop out was finalized after a few quick signatures.

Rent

As I drove to my house, I was careful to avoid any ice on the roads, and watched my fellow drivers who, thankfully, were just as cautious as I was. I had to come up with a reasonable excuse to offer the house to Jason, one that didn't include Salem. Would he believe me if I said I was living with Paul? I contemplated that possibility as I pulled into my driveway, finding Jason was already there waiting. There was a layer of slush covering the ground and sidewalk that led to the door.

"Hey, Jason!" I yelled as I opened my car door. I was about to step out onto the slush when he hurried over, took my hand and helped me steadily through it. "Thanks." I chuckled. "Can't afford to be slipping and breaking my skull."

"Yeah, wouldn't want you to end up in a cast like me." He laughed and my eyes fell upon the white bandage wrapped around his arm.

"Not bad enough to need a sling?" I inquired as I unlocked the front door.

"Nope, thankfully. Those things look so uncomfortable," he grumbled. "Not to say this is comfortable, and man does it itch."

"I'm really sorry that happened, Jace." I frowned and let him lead me into the house.

I switched on the dining room light and was still unimpressed by the place in comparison to Salem's amazing house. I tossed my keys onto the table and went to offer Jason a drink when I realized in horror how long ago I had bought food. I also spotted the glass with the dying daffodils in it that Jason had given me; I hoped he wouldn't notice them, but it was somewhat inevitable.

"Smells kind of funny in here," he commented as I ran frantically to the fridge.

As soon as I opened it, I gagged. All of the food I had purchased had spoiled.

"Wow ... " I sighed. "Sorry you had to see, and smell, this."

"It's okay." He laughed. "How long has it been since you stayed here?"

"A while. I've been," I paused, thinking it over, "I've been staying with Paul."

"Really? That's nice of him to take you in like that and help you out while you've been sick and all. Wish I had an uncle that nice. My mom's brothers are crazy! Want me to help you clear that out?"

"Are you sure you're okay to help, with your ... " I pointed to his injured arm.

"Yeah, no problem, I still have one good one, you know." He smirked.

The next hour was spent disposing of the rotten food, cleaning the fridge, and leaving it open to air out. I ordered a pizza and pocketed the remaining money that Janet had left me. Jason was shocked when I told him what had caused her untimely death—although, it wasn't entirely true. My story involved her being bitten by the bear at the zoo, and getting a terrible infection from it that spread quickly to her heart—I hated lying to him, especially about something so serious, but overall I knew it was the best thing to do.

The pizza delivery man showed up just in time to interrupt any responses from Jason on the story behind Janet's death. Jason and I sat in silence for a few minutes when I abruptly sat down my slice of pizza and looked up at him.

"How are things going over at Howard's?" I asked as casually as possible.

"Great. I got a raise last week!" he exclaimed after swallowing his food.

"That's good news." I smiled. "There's something important I need to talk to you about."

He looked slightly uncomfortable now, if not a little worried. "It's not about the other day at the diner, is it?"

"Not entirely, but it's got to do with something you told me while we were there," I replied, tapping my fingers nervously on the table as I recalled that afternoon. "How are your parents doing?"

Jason stopped eating and sighed. "The arguments are getting even worse, and to the point that Mitchell and I wind up sleeping outside in my car to avoid the noise some nights."

"That's horrible," I said, noticing the sadness in his eyes. "What would you say if I offered you my house, for a very low rent?"

His expression perked up slightly. "As a roommate?"

● ● ●

I laughed and shook my head. "No, though that is a tempting idea. I think I'm going to just stick with living with Paul for now ... he gets lonely."

"Oh. Then, just me?"

"You could bring Mitchell, too, if you like ... or whoever else. Just as long as you keep it safe and clean."

"Wow." He smiled really big, exposing his straight, white teeth. "That would be awesome, Alex! Are you sure you'd want to do that?"

"Yeah ... there's nothing left for me here now, besides bad memories." I sighed. "I thought about selling it, but then decided to ask you first if you'd be interested in it at all."

"I would be more than happy to take it!" He grinned again. "Imagine the parties ... "

I shook my head, laughing. "I had a feeling you might say that."

"How much were you thinking ... for rent?"

"I really don't want any of your money, actually," I said, shrugging. "All I want is to know it's taken care of, and I can come by whenever I need to."

He blinked. "You are going to let me stay for free?"

"Yeah. You're my best friend, Jason. I can't take your money." I smiled at him, "You'll have to pay the rest of the bills though of course, and some land taxes once a year, but aside from that it'll be free."

"This is unbelievable, Alex!" He leapt from his chair and gave me a one-armed hug and an unexpected peck on the cheek. I was secretly glad it wasn't more than that. "Don't be surprised if you get some money from me now and then, though. I don't want to feel like I am taking advantage of you! When can I move in?"

"Anytime. If you want, we can take out the furniture, and you can replace it with your own, or you can just keep it … or sell it. I really don't care."

"Are you serious?" He gaped at me, examining the surroundings. "You can't imagine how grateful I am, Alex … and Mitchell will love it, too!"

"I'm glad. I just have one other condition … " I said suddenly.

"What is it? I'll do anything!"

"Don't tell Paul … he wouldn't understand."

"Sure, I won't say a word about it." He grinned and hugged me again. "I'm going to go home and tell Mitch. Mom should be relieved to have us out of there, too. That way, we aren't there to see and hear the arguing and fighting anymore."

I smiled, grateful that he was happy, and that I would no longer have the burden of tending to the place—not that I did a good job of that. "Tell Mitchell I said hi. Try not to spend too much time fighting over bedrooms."

Jason laughed. "I've got a feeling it won't be too hard. Thanks so much Alex!"

"You're welcome," I said, gave him a set of house keys and walked out with him. He took my hand and guided me to my car to protect me from the slush again, and before long I was pulling out of the driveway, and he was walking home, both of us headed in different directions.

The Grave

I scoured the local cemetery that night, despite not hearing any rumors of bizarre behavior in the vicinity. I was positive I had not eliminated every vile vampire in town, and I had a strange feeling that I might encounter one here tonight. Before arriving, I called Salem to let him know where I would be, and I knew that before long he would show up—whether visible or in hiding. The snow and slush had all but dissipated, leaving a thick layer of mud on the ground. The brown sludge was thick against the base of my sneakers. My crossbow was concealed beneath my dark jacket, the lump only noticeable if you were actually looking for it.

The area was completely quiet, giving it a creepy vibe—as if an old graveyard wasn't disturbing enough already. I passed through a section of near-identical headstones, idly reading the names and dates as I walked by each one:

Henry Eddison – 1954 – 1986.
Jeffery Leonard – 1936 – 2000.
Marcy Wickman – 2000 – 2006.

The last one overwhelmed me. Only six years of life ... my lips curved downward, and I tried to ignore the oncoming depressive thoughts until my eyes met the grave marker beside Marcy's. It looked new, as if it had just been placed recently. In fact, had I taken another step forward I would have collapsed into the vacant grave. Hesitantly, I peered downward—it was empty. My curiosity got the best of me—as it often had—and I crouched beside the headstone to get a look at the name.

It was difficult to read in the dark, unlike the older ones I had read just seconds ago; these letters were black. My hand began trembling as I traced my index finger along the inscription. As my eyes adjusted, the letters came into view, and I gasped. Big, bold letters ran across the front of the stone:

ALEXIS WALDRON
SEPTEMBER 9, 1994 – NOVEMBER 13, 2012

I jumped away from what was presumably *my* grave and bumped into something—someone. I shouted and tried to run, but a cold hand wrapped around my arm. I sighed with relief.

"Salem?" I said in a hopeful voice. "Please tell me that's you."

"I am afraid not, my dear." The voice was unfamiliar, masculine and dark. It did, however, hold a similar accent to that of Salem's.

My body involuntarily shuddered, though not at all from the gust of wind that swept passed us. He spun me around with the slightest movement of his hand, and I came face to face with my assailant. His face seemed almost gentle. He must have been in his mid-thirties, before he became a member of the undead. His eyes were circled with deep, purple shadows, and the irises were a surprisingly cool shade of amber. A mane of pale blonde hair cascaded down to his shoulders, and his lips were arched in a dreadful grin that stole away any beauty that may have existed on his face.

"You cannot begin to imagine how long it has been since I waited for this moment." His cold, smooth hand swept the side of my face. "Once word of a raven caught my attention, I simply had to come to this little hole of a town to meet her! And for it to be *you*, of all people!" He laughed darkly, but I didn't understand the humor.

"Where did you hear that from?" I gasped at his touch, while attempting to keep my voice level and not show my fear. Where was Salem when I needed him!

"I have my connections. However, that is unimportant, Alexis. What is important, is what I am about to offer you." His hand fell upon my throat, but his touch was gentle, without intent to hurt me—yet.

"There is nothing I could ever want from a monster like you!" I shouted, squirming to get away but despite how gentle he was holding me I couldn't break free.

He shut his eyes and shook his head slowly from side to side, making a 'tsk-tsk' sound. "You really shouldn't lie to me like that, dear Alexis." His eyes opened, revealing empty black voids. My jaw fell open when I saw Salem's face reflected in his pupils. "I am fully aware of your relationship with a 'monster' such as I, and I know he would hate to hear you call him one."

"Salem isn't a monster." My voice was low and steady, very much unlike my heartbeat.

"Then, why should I be classified as one?" He grinned again and I could see the tips of his pearly fangs. "That truly hurts my feelings." His voice was overly sarcastic.

"I doubt you even have feelings!" I shouted, wriggling in his grasp once more – this time he tightened his hold on me.

The vampire cocked his head to the side and looked at me, examining me from head to toe. "Let's get back to my offer, now, shall we?"

"Spit it out already!"

He smiled fully then, and I was amazed at how stunning he looked with the moonlight casting a radiant glow against his blonde hair. "I have never personally met a Waldron that could turn into a raven; this is truly a treat for me! And, to have one in my arms, so warm and wriggling ... it is most tempting. I could kill you right now, and no one would ever know where to find you. However!" He paused dramatically, leaning his head toward my throat. I could hear him inhaling my scent. "What if I offered you everlasting life? It is what you wish for, is it not?"

"Are you asking to make me, a vampire hunter ... into a vampire?" I almost laughed. But he was far from being wrong with his assumption on my want for immortality.

"That is precisely what I am offering you, Alexis Waldron! Never having to worry about aging, isn't that what you want?" His voice was alluring. "Imagine, being with your beloved Salem without having to worry about age or death ever coming between you! Considering he doesn't appear willing to grant you your desires, I thought perhaps I would offer."

"Death is still possible." My voice was a mere whisper. "My family is evidence enough of that."

"Your family has never been the best of hunters, aside from a few and perhaps yourself. You show potential at being so much more, however."

"That's why you want me, then, isn't it?"

His gaze met mine, and he smirked. "You are also quite intelligent, but are you smart enough to make the right decision? As a vampire, you could be so powerful, so capable. By my side, we could take control of the infantile vampires; teach them the proper ways of hunting. Imagine the endless supply of blood we could gather, town after town!" His malicious laughter sent chills down my spine. "Tell me this does not tempt you, my darling Alexis?"

My mind was racing with questions, worries, wonders, the possibilities ... how would Salem react to this? Would he love me less if I accepted this vampire's proposal? Would I become a monster, or would I be capable of controlling my want – my need – to feast on human blood?

"Salem's opinion is not important," the vampire murmured, his cold lips right below my ear. "All that matters now is this moment, this decision." It was hard to resist the hypnotic tone of his voice as it whispered against my throat.

"And if I say no?"

He shrugged his shoulders and let out a wisp of laughter. "Then, I shall enjoy your blood thoroughly before discarding your empty corpse in this pit beside us."

"That sure gives me a lot of options," I groaned. "Before I make any decisions, answer me one thing," I offered, hoping to buy me some time. Surely, Salem would be here soon.

The blonde-haired vampire arched a curious brow. "What have you to ask of me, raven?"

"Who are you and how did you know where to find me?"

He didn't release me, but loosened his grasp on my arm. "How I found you is simple. I have a direct connection with your Salem, although he might not be aware of that. We have somewhat of a ... bond, you might say, as do all vampires and their Sires." His mouth formed a malicious grin, and my eyes grew wide.

"Raziel ... "

"Ah, so he *has* mentioned me! How delightful," Raziel mused as he brushed his fingers through my hair, despite my obvious objection to his gesture. "Now, was that all you wanted to know or may we get through with this? You must understand how difficult it is for me, mere inches from you ... the blood coursing through your veins nearly beckons to me! I don't understand how Salem can tolerate it."

"Because he can control himself—something that all of you should learn to do!"

"That leads me to believe you are not going to accept my offer." He frowned. "You would have made such a wonderful addition to the family."

"My own family would hunt me down and kill me eventually."

"Not necessarily. Do you realize how long I have walked this earth without a single brush with death?" Raziel laughed. I could feel his breath against my skin. "I could teach you the proper ways of being a vampire. The ones you have killed are mere fledglings without guidance!"

This was not how I imagined my death, helpless in a graveyard with a vampire. But what choice did I have? I couldn't bear to live for all eternity with Salem loathing me for what I had become, or worse still— becoming a monster like the one in front of me. "I can't accept your offer ... " I said quietly, feeling the tears well up in the corner of my eyes.

Raziel sighed against my cheek. "You have greatly disappointed me, dear raven ... and your beloved Salem, no doubt." He laughed mockingly. "I would have thought you had his best interest in mind!"

"This would be his best interest!" I shouted. "He wouldn't want me to be like you!"

The vampire shook his head once more. "Your answers astound me, but very well." My eyes widened in horror as he flung my body to the ground. I heard something crack as I hit the side of a tombstone. Why was I not transforming?! I could fly away; I could escape this brutal torture! And where the hell was Salem!

I struggled to get up then realized with anguished screams that it was no use—my leg was either fractured or broken. Raziel laughed as I shook with pain on the muddy surface, his body looming over me. I saw his once-amber eyes flood with darkness. With one sudden, swift motion, he was on top of me, his hands pressed into mine. I thought he was about to end it all, but instead I saw something reflected in his eyes. Images played like a movie through his pupils, and suddenly I was engulfed in the darkness as though dragged into the scene of a movie.

Visions

My eyes quickly scanned the area. I was in a small house decorated in plain, dull furnishings. The living room was cramped with a small sofa, a rocking chair and an old bassinet. To the left of me was a kitchen that looked extremely outdated, and realization struck me: Raziel was sharing a memory with me. My legs took me down a small hall and into a room on the right. I wasn't in control of my movements; the vampire must have been guiding me.

The room was bright and colorful, with a small bed in the corner and another rocking chair beside it. I gasped at the sight of the adorable little girl curled up in the bed. A braid of golden hair lay delicately across her sleeping face. She looked serene, until her eyes flew open. I worried that she had seen me, but realized there was no way that was possible. Someone else was in the room with me. I turned to see a tall figure hiding in the shadows. His eyes glimmered like amber jewels, and I knew at once who I was seeing.

"Daniel!" Hannah's angelic voice whispered when she saw him. "I'm so happy to see you!"

Daniel? This couldn't be right. The man stepped out of the shadows, wiping away all doubt. This was Raziel's face. The eyes, the blonde hair, the gentle features—there was no mistaking him.

"Hannah, my love!" He smiled and lifted the small child into his arms. "I have missed you so."

"Momma says that you are imaginary, Daniel," the little girl said as she hugged the man. "Is that true?"

The man laughed. "Of course it isn't. If I were imaginary, I couldn't possibly be holding you. You would be floating!"

A flood of harmonious giggles filled the room. How had no one else heard the sound? Perhaps the Young family was so used to hearing Hannah talk and laugh with herself at night that it no longer woke them. The bond between her and Daniel was beautiful, yet it somehow sickened me.

"I brought you a present," Daniel said with a sly grin. "But you must keep it a secret."

"Okay!" Hannah said joyfully, anticipating the surprise.

Daniel pulled a locket from the pocket of his brown vest and offered it to the child. "I bought this especially for you," he said and his face lit up at the girl's reaction. "Let me put it on for you."

I watched as the man placed Hannah on the floor and gently wound the necklace around her neck. She pulled it up to her face and pried open the locket. There was a small black-and-white picture of her on one side, the other was empty.

"Why isn't there a picture of you in here?" she asked.

"I don't photograph well," he replied with a light laugh.

"Or you really are imaginary!" Hannah said with a gasp.

"Perhaps." Daniel smiled sadly. "There is one more thing I have for you, dear Hannah. Can you promise that you will give it to your mother in the morning?"

"Of course!"

"Good girl," he said and offered her a folded piece of paper. "Make sure *daddy* isn't around when she reads it," he warned, emphasizing unpleasantly on the word 'daddy', and then patted her lightly on the head.

"Okay!" She hugged Daniel and kissed him gently on the cheek.

"Time for bed then," he said, picking her up and gently placing her on the tiny mattress. He pulled the covers up and tucked her in. "I'll be back tomorrow night."

"Promise?" she said with a pout.

"Promise." He smiled and disappeared out the window.

The vision faded and another appeared. I was now outside, peering in through a window. Daniel was beside me, discreetly hidden so that he wouldn't be caught peeping. Hannah and Maggie were sitting together on the rocking chair in the living room; our view of them was from the side. Their voices came through the window as if we were right beside them.

"What is it, Hannah?" Maggie asked as the small girl offered her a piece of paper.

"Daniel asked me to give this to you."

Maggie's eyes grew angry at the name, but she relaxed somewhat and sighed. "How many times must I tell you that he is not real, darling?"

"He *is* real!" Hannah argued.

Maggie ignored her daughter and unfolded the paper.
I suspect she had been anticipating a letter covered in
childish scribbles or nothing at all—instead she found a note
scrawled in magnificent lettering. I could barely read the
letters from where I was. But, I could distinctly hear
Margaret's voice as if she was reading it aloud, although her
lips never moved.

"Dearest Margaret,
Despite your regrets and frequent requests that I
cease to visit my dear Hannah, I am afraid I cannot abide
by your rules. She is mine just as much as she is yours.
Come to your senses and please tell Arthur the truth. Tell
Hannah the truth! She deserves to know who her true father
is. It pains me to be away from her, and for you to try to
convince her that I am unreal is preposterous!
Please, if you cared for me at all, you would do this
for me—for us.
With love – whether returned or forgotten,
Thomas D. Winter"

Before I had the opportunity to even think about what
I had just seen, I was dragged into another memory. Daniel
was weak and drunk, slumped against the wall of an alley.
His eyes were red and swollen from tears, and he looked
younger than before. His face was flushed and red, full of
life—he wasn't a vampire in this vision. Clenched in his hand
hung a crumpled piece of paper that had obviously been read
countless times, judging by the state of it. His voice entered
my head as he re-read the note:

"Thomas,

I did not know how to tell you this in person. I am with child. It is unlikely—no—it is impossible that this child is Arthur's. It is yours, Tom. I know that we had planned to set off together, and that I would leave him, but things have changed; we have reconciled. I cannot do this to Salem or Arthur. I will raise this baby as his, and it will never even know your name. I am sorry Thomas, but you must understand. This is for the best, for us all.
Farewell,
Margaret."

After one last swig of alcohol, he tossed the bottle furiously at the wall across from him. The bottle shattered and sprinkled tiny pieces of sharp glass all around. His eyes were suddenly alert to the sound of footsteps.

"Who's there?" he asked with a drunken slur.

No one replied. I watched as a woman with bright-red eyes stalked toward him, knelt beside him and frowned at his pitiful appearance.

"What's the matter, doll?" she said with false interest.

"Nothin' important," he grumbled.

"I can take away all of your agony," she offered, taking his chin in her hand. "Would that be ideal for you?"

He simply nodded his head. He regretted his response immediately when the woman bared her fangs and sank them into the flesh of his throat. His screams were unbearable; he thrashed around in agony as she meant to drain him completely.

"Please ... " he whispered hoarsely. "Just let me die."

The woman's eyes fell upon his pleading lips, and she laughed, "A beggar, are we?" I watched a trickle of blood run down her chin. As she went to take his life away, a sudden sound disrupted her, and she left him lying limply in the alley.

I was at the house again, staring in through the same window. My heart leapt at the sight of Salem; his appearance was the same as I knew it to be now. He was sitting on the floor with Hannah, playing with a small black cat. Daniel was beside me once more, his appearance different from that in the alley. His cheeks were no longer flushed. His skin was ashen, and his amber eyes had a ring of crimson around them. My gaze was averted as I heard an unfamiliar male's voice.

Arthur entered the room and requested that Salem and Hannah retreat to their bedrooms. His expression was calm, but I could see the hurt in his eyes. Once their children were out of the room, Margaret appeared behind him. She looked withdrawn, and her eyes showed evidence of recent tears.

"How could you do this to me, Maggie—to our family?!" Arthur's accent reminded me vaguely of his son's. "When? When did this happen?"

"I-I cannot remember exactly, Arthur," Maggie sobbed. "It wasn't intentional—we were having trouble and ... and things got out of hand. Please, you must forgive me!"

Her husband was raging; his fists clenched tightly beside him. "You betrayed me in the worst way!"

"I am sorry, Arthur!"

I wanted to look away, but I was forced to watch. Arthur's fist swiftly met Maggie's cheek. She cried in pain, recoiling from him.

"Arthur!" she screamed. "Please! Do not do this! The children will hear!"

Beside me, Daniel was obviously furious—and perhaps ashamed. I could sense his urgency to protect Maggie, to stop the inevitable brawl between husband and wife, but he couldn't. It would have only made the situation worse.

Arthur's hand met Maggie's cheek once more, and this time she fell to the floor. She curled up in a ball and started sobbing hysterically. Her husband deserted her, leaving through the front door.

The memory I least wanted to see came flooding through my mind. Arthur and Maggie were on better terms. They each slept in the same room, in separate beds. I walked out of their bedroom and down the hall. There was a small fire burning unnoticed in the kitchen. I desperately longed to put it out, to save Salem the grief of what had happened to his family—but it was impossible. My eyes stared in horror as the flames grew higher and higher. They licked at the walls, the furniture, and the beautiful rocking chair. I was standing in the middle of the fire, unharmed as the flames weaved their way down the hall.

I ran along the hallway, into Hannah's room where the fire was starting to crawl. Daniel was standing outside her window, looking in. I wondered if he had set the blaze, but the vision did not answer. Once he saw the orange hues illuminating the open doorway he slammed through the window and went to retrieve her.

"Daniel!" she shouted happily in a tired voice as he plucked her quickly from her bed. "I thought you would never come back!" She frowned. "What is it, Daniel?"

Daniel hesitated and flinched at the sight of the girl's half-brother curled up on the floor beside her bed. "What is he doing in here, Hannah?" he said in a rushed voice.

• • •

"I had a nightmare after mommy and daddy fought last night." Daniel cringed at the word 'daddy'; I was amazed by how much pain it caused him. "So Salem stayed with me."

Salem muttered something to Hannah about going back to sleep, and then realized someone else was present. He screamed at the sight of the pale figure in his sister's room.

"Get out of our house!" Salem yelled, it was the same beautiful voice I had grown to love. Daniel paused abruptly, prepared to escape the house with Hannah, but Salem had distracted him.

"I will not leave without her!" he yelled, cradling her in his arms. "You ... you weren't supposed to be in here."

"Salem!" Hannah yelled. "Look!"

Salem turned toward where the girl pointed, and stepped back in horror as the fire swept across the wooden floorboards. He averted his eyes from the flames when he heard Hannah screaming, but to his dismay, she was already gone through the broken window along with Daniel. The fire grew around him, licking away the floor beneath him. His cries of agony filled my ears—I could barely withstand it. I watched as he forced himself through the burning flames and out through Hannah's window.

● ● ●

Raziel

I thought another vision was coming when I heard Salem's voice, but I was mistaken. The weight upon me was lifted, and Raziel was nowhere to be seen.

"I was beginning to wonder if you would ever show up." Raziel laughed. I lifted my head in search of him. He was getting up from the ground, wiping the corner of his mouth. I realized in horror that my neck was moist ... my fingers found the spot, and I gasped in horror. The visions had all just been a distraction. Salem was too late ... I was dying; there was nothing he could do for me now.

My eyes found Salem, crouched behind a tombstone. He glanced at me briefly, his eyes full of despair, then focused on Raziel. "What have you done to her, Raziel?!" he demanded.

"I hadn't quite had the chance to finish ... she was nearly mine!" he fumed. "For a raven she was quite easy to trick." His laughter filled my ears.

"You didn't ... " Salem's voice was cut off as Raziel leapt at him, shoving him against a tree. The blonde-haired fiend slid his icy fingers around Salem's throat and grinned.

• • •

"I thought you would be stronger than this, Salem." He frowned. "What have you been up to all these years? I admit, I used to keep an eye on you after you left, but I could only stand seeing you suckle on rabbits so much. Such a pity. I wasted so much time on you."

Salem shoved him away with little effort. "You underestimate me," he growled and pinned him to the ground. "Tell me you didn't turn her!"

Raziel grinned up at him. "No, I didn't get that far ... but she won't live much longer, so it matters little now."

"I'll save her."

"Just like you saved your beloved sister." Raziel smirked. With the love he had shown in those visions, how could he speak of her like that?

"How do you know any of that?"

"*I was there.*" Raziel laughed once more. "You don't remember, do you?"

"No ... " Salem's voice trailed off as he stared transfixed into Raziel's eyes. I knew immediately what was happening—he was relaying a memory to Salem.

"Daniel ... " His voice was distant; he was still trapped in the memory. Suddenly, he let out a blood-curdling scream.

The crunching, snapping, twisting sound came all at once. I was above them, a twirl of feathers spinning on the ground below me. My leg was still undoubtedly broken, but the rest of my body felt at ease now. My mouth fell open in a loud outburst. Salem collapsed off of Raziel's body, both of them covering their ears at the piercing sound. I soared downward and perched myself on Raziel's shoulders. My beak met his flesh, and he flung his hand at me. The poison didn't appear to be weakening him in the slightest; in fact, he appeared mildly amused.

I was soaring again, but this time it was not intentional. My avian body slammed into a nearby tree, and I crumbled to the ground. My body convulsed again, and I acknowledged that I was no longer a raven. When my eyes were able to focus again, I screamed. Raziel had Salem pinned to the ground, a devious grin across his ashen lips.

"You could never imagine what I saw in her memories and future," he said as he held Salem firmly still. "It is so unfortunate that you will never know what could become of her and of her abilities ... and your future together."

"She isn't going to die," Salem snarled, fighting against Raziel's strength.

The older vampire shook his head in pity. "There is no sense in fighting, my child. You are weaker than I, and you always will be unless you start living like a real vampire. Animal blood might be able to sustain you, but it will never give you the strength, the power, which human blood can."

"I'm not interested in power! You should have just left me to die rather than turn me into this monster!"

"You do not mean that." As he spoke, I saw a glint of silver extracted from the pocket of the brown vest he wore. "I had my reasons to keep you as alive as possible. I had such high hopes for you, dearest Salem. You were young, clever, and had so much potential. I suffered much anguish after you deserted me, but it wasn't because of my own feelings." He smirked. "There is so much you missed out on. If you had known the truth, you would be begging me to take you back, begging to go back in time to be reunited."

"What are you talking about?" Salem asked, a hint of fear in his voice, but I couldn't perceive why.

"It is not my place to explain, and with how tonight's events are turning out, you might very well never know."

"Wait!" Salem protested—against what I wasn't sure. "How did you know where to find Alexis?"

"A Sire has a direct connection to that of his offspring. I can look into your thoughts and memories as if I was inside your very mind," he explained. "Not every Sire possesses this ability, or perhaps is not aware of how to access it ... but that scarcely matters anymore. None of this information will matter in the next few seconds. It is such a pity, dearest Salem ... " He sighed and spoke almost affectionately. "I will always remember you as being my first. But enough of that, I am going to enjoy carving out your pathetic heart."

Salem's screams reached my ears immediately, and I struggled to stand until the sharp pain in my leg reminded me that I was helpless. With some relief, I felt myself becoming the raven once more, but I barely had enough strength left to hover even a few feet off of the ground. Raziel blocked Salem from my view, and while I didn't want to hurt him, my mouth fell open and the cemetery was filled with the loud, piercing sound of my caw once again. The source of the silver glint I had seen moments earlier was lying beside Salem—a short, curved dagger painted with vibrant red blood.

Raziel trembled at the sound, his ghastly hands cupping over his ears. My gaze fell upon Salem, and my heart sank. His head was to the side; his serene face masked in splatters of blood and grime, his eyes shut tightly. A deep gash ran across his chest, but I knew he wasn't dead. Somehow I knew that if he was, I would have felt it—or at least I had hoped. The caw filled the air again and Raziel faltered, and I watched Salem's eyes flicker open.

My strength was waning, and I felt myself crash to the ground once more. With what little energy I had left, I watched the scene before me as I felt my eyelids drooping.

Salem, despite the wound in his chest and obvious agony he was in, gathered himself from the ground and tackled Raziel into the nearest gravestone. Fighting the urge to shut my eyes, I could see his fangs bared against his Sire's throat.

His voice played through my mind from a distant memory. *"Raziel is more important to you alive. If you kill him, you kill me, and any other vampires he created."*

"No, Salem!" I cried, although I wasn't sure it was loud enough that he could hear me. "Don't!"

He ignored my ill-attempt to stop him, if he even heard it at all. I shut my eyes tightly and felt the moist tears trickle down my cheeks. Raziel's blood-chilling scream made me shudder, and I covered my ears awaiting the most painful sound I could imagine: the sound of Salem screaming as he too died. It never came.

"Clearly ... " Raziel's voice broke through the screaming, "I did underestimate you ... "

I was reluctant at first, but slowly I let the darkness swallow me.

"Alexis. Wake up, please ... " Salem's voice begged from the shadows. I opened my eyes and smiled at his flawless face.

"I knew heaven would be beautiful," I mumbled.

"Heaven?" Salem shook his head. "You're not in heaven, Alex."

My brows furrowed. "What did I do to deserve to go to Hell?"

He shook his head again and lifted me into his arms. "You aren't dead."

"I must be. Raziel killed me. You killed him, and that killed you." I stated this as though it were a fact.

• • •

"No, Alex ... " his expression grew worried. "You didn't die; you were close, but you definitely didn't die. And as it turns out, Raziel's tale of killing one's Sire must have been just another way to keep his 'offspring' at bay."

"How am I not dead?"

"I intervened before he had the chance to kill you, remember?" he replied tenderly, brushing a strand of hair from my face. "It was almost too late ... "

"You saved me." I smiled weakly. "Oh, Salem ... the things he showed me ... "

"I know," he whispered, pulling me against him. "Hannah didn't die in the fire. I had been so certain she had ... the memory of her dying had been so vivid, almost as if a false memory had been planted in my mind."

I would have thought he would have been pleased by that news, but from the look of disgust and pain on his face, I was unsure. "Why doesn't that comfort you?"

"He killed her," he replied through clenched teeth.

"No!" I gasped, "No. He loved her."

Salem frowned. "Daniel may have loved her, but Raziel did not. He showed me something, something I gather wasn't shared with you. He tried to live with her, tried to tend to her, but failed. The monster in him couldn't handle it. Daniel was dead long before he—Raziel—killed Hannah."

"Why did he change his name to Raziel?" I wondered aloud.

"Possibly to help forget who he once was." He shrugged. "Hannah demanded that he come back and save me ... but I don't think she understood what he would have to do to 'save' me."

"Yet, you never saw her at all?"

"Not that I can recall. He must have been keeping her somewhere else ... " He shook the memories from his head for a moment and focused his gaze back to me.

"You were so willing ... to die for me," I said quietly, wincing as he examined my leg.

"Of course, I was," he replied gently then lowered me onto the muddied ground. He crumbled my gravestone into pieces with one swift kick. I stared at him in awe as he pushed Raziel's body into the pit that had been originally intended for me. Salem's eyes flashed purple and a mound of dirt appeared, filling the hole.

"Your wound ... " I whispered hoarsely. "Is it healed?"

"Not yet, but that's not important. Let's get you to a doctor. You have lost a lot of blood, and need your leg checked out," he said as he lifted me up once more.

Recovery

I had thought the fracture in my leg was the worst of the damage, but I was mistaken. It was amazing how oblivious I was to the severe blood loss. The trip to the hospital was a mystery to me; Salem explained that I had passed out along the way and was unconscious for nearly three days. The doctor had given me a blood transfusion to recover some of the lost fluid – he assumed it was caused from the severe gashes in my leg and Salem, nor I bothered to tell him otherwise. He was, however, somewhat skeptical about the bizarre bite mark on my throat. I insisted I was bit by an animal during an afternoon hike and fallen down an embankment, but he seemed unconvinced. They ran a few tests to ensure I wasn't infected with any diseases from the bite, and all the results were clear. I was just grateful that they released me. I loathed hospitals almost as much as I hated gym class. When I exited the hospital room, donning my new set of metal crutches, I was shocked to find Paul sitting in the waiting room. My instincts told me to retreat and walk in the other direction, but it was too late – he had seen me.

"Alex, please don't go!" He stood up from the plastic chair and rushed to my side. "I know we've been on rough terms lately, but I had to see you."

"How did you even know I was here?" I grumbled, leaning my weight uncomfortably on the crutch the doctor had provided.

"Salem called me, actually ... " He stared down at his feet. "This would be the second time he saved your life. I think I owe him an apology, Alex."

"Well, I'm glad you finally got that through your thick skull."

"I'm trying to be civil here. Could you at least try to hear me out?" He sighed with frustration.

"Whatever, Paul." I didn't meet his eyes. "You'll at least be glad to know Raziel is dead—also thanks to Salem."

"He told me all about that, too." He sighed. "This isn't going to be easy for me, Alex, but I think over time I can come to accept your relationship with him."

My eyes finally met his. "Are you serious?"

He nodded his head slowly. "I think so, anyway. I never imagined a vampire could feel so strongly for a human, but I can see—and hear—he way he cares about you."

"He's more in touch with his human half than the vampire in him," I said as Paul opened the hospital doors for me.

My face brightened when I saw Salem leaning against the side of the building, drenched in the pouring rain. The moisture plastered his ebony hair to his scalp, and beads of water trickled down his pale face. He looked relieved to see me, but a little anxious at Paul's presence. Surprisingly, to both of us, Paul offered my arm to Salem. My father took one of my crutches so that Salem could intertwine his cold arm with mine, and he led me to the Wrangler parked far off into the lot.

When we were in the car, Salem sat in the back with me, holding my hand tightly in his. Paul peeked back at us, a smug look on his face. I began to worry if he had sincerely meant he was going to try to accept our relationship. As we rode along the street, I leaned my head tiredly against Salem's cold, wet shoulder and shut my eyes.

I was barely asleep when I heard the voices—part of me was unsure if I was conscious or not.

"I think I owe you an apology, Salem," Paul muttered, barely audible over the rush of wind and splattering rain against the windshield.

"You are forgiven," he muttered in response, caressing my hair gently. "I understand your reasons."

"It's not going to be easy to get used to."

"I understand that, too," Salem replied in a hushed voice, obviously not wanting to disturb me.

"Salem," Paul spoke just as quietly. "I give you the benefit of the doubt, but if you ever so much as scratch her ... well, let's just say I won't miss next time."

"You have nothing to worry about."

My eyes barely opened when the car pulled to a stop outside of the Victorian. Salem nudged me gently on the shoulder in an attempt to wake me. "We're home," he whispered into my ear.

I sat up and stretched my stiffened arms, smiling happily at the sight of the welcoming doors. Salem helped me out of the car and acted as my support, leading me up the alabaster stairs slowly and steadily.

"You are welcome to come inside, Paul," he hollered back at my father who still sat in the Jeep, his expression blank.

He hesitated before leaving the vehicle and following us into the glorious house. A shimmer of regret crossed his face as he eyed the stained-glass windows on the door. As he opened his mouth to speak, Salem silenced him.

"I know. You are sorry for the windows, also."

"You can't read minds, can you?" Paul laughed darkly.

"No." Salem smirked, looking back at Paul. "You're just somewhat predictable."

"Which is why I've never been able to kill you, I guess," Paul grumbled.

"Dad!" I shouted. "That's enough."

"Sorry, Alex. Old habits die hard, y'know?" Paul frowned. "But I'm tryin'."

"Thank you. That is all I ask for."

"What would you like to eat, my little raven?" Salem asked as he lowered me onto the sectional. His eyes twinkled violet momentarily, and a plump pillow appeared in his hands. He gently placed my fractured leg against the pillow. I smiled gratefully, and watched my father gaze around the house. He was clearly mesmerized. But who could blame him?

"I'll have whatever Paul wants," I said with a sly grin.

Salem looked uneasy. "I'm not sure that's such a good idea, Alex," he muttered.

"What isn't? Paul asked as he entered the vast living room. He was momentarily distracted by the white grand piano in the corner. "Ah, I see what she really likes about you."

Salem laughed delicately.

"Dad, if you could have anything to eat right now – what would it be?" I asked, ignoring them.

"Steak and a baked potato!" he answered quickly. "Why? Does Salem have his own chef to go with this mansion of a house or something?" he scoffed.

"Not exactly, no." I grinned. "Go on, Salem ... "

Salem frowned at me, then I saw the mystical purple highlights in his eyes, and he gestured for Paul to look into the dining room. Upon the dining table were two plates, each with a steaming hot potato with all the toppings imaginable nestled beside a large steak. My father stared in awe at the food, his jaw gaping open.

"How?" he mumbled; his eyes focused now on Salem.

"There is more to me than just being a vampire." Salem grimaced somewhat.

Paul shook his head in disbelief. "Amazing ... " he whispered. "What else can you do?"

"That's about it."

I smiled to myself, happy to see they were getting along—at least a little, anyway. Salem brought me my plate and helped me sit up. "Thank you," I said and pecked him on the cheek while Paul delved into his meal. I picked at mine, somewhat wishing I had chosen something of my own—steak wasn't among my favorite foods, but the potato was delicious.

"Salem?" I said quietly, eying my dad in the kitchen. "Did you have any idea about Hannah being Daniel—Raziel's daughter?"

He shook his head and scowled. "That's not something I ever expected ... I don't even want to think about it."

"What do you think he meant by all that stuff he said to you?"

"I don't know, Alex ... " He sighed, appearing thoughtful. "Perhaps I never will quite understand that, now."

"And ... My future." I gasped. "What do you suppose he saw?"

"I don't know that, either ... but we will have plenty of time to find out."

After I finished my meal, I grudgingly let sleep overcome me as my father asked Salem all about his bizarre summoning abilities.

Nevermore

When I awoke the next morning, Paul was gone and Salem was nowhere to be seen. I sighed heavily with disappointment; I wouldn't be able to get up on my own and would have to wait for Salem to return from wherever he happened to be. As I thought this over, the front doors flew open, and he was walking gracefully through them. He came to my side at once and pulled me into his arms.

"Do you need anything?" he asked, staring at my injured leg remorsefully.

"I could use help getting to the bathroom," I groaned, knowing this would include him carrying me upstairs. "What were you doing outside?"

"I was saying farewell to your father. He stayed throughout the night to ensure you were okay." He smiled, lifted me into his arms and rushed me up the spiraling stairs. He helped me through the restroom door, and I insisted I could take care of the rest myself, although I wasn't completely sure of that. I could hear him shuffling around behind the door while he waited for me. I took care of the persistent nagging of my bladder, washed my hands, and then quickly brushed my teeth, leaning against the counter for support.

He was waiting with his arms outstretched and a wide smile when I opened the door. I allowed him to carry me down the stairs but was surprised when he didn't take me to the sofa. Instead, he swung my legs over the bench in front of the piano and sat beside me. I looked at him inquisitively as he placed his hands over mine and guided them to the keys.

"Play that tune for me, one more time," he requested after kissing me softly.

"Okay." I breathed and flexed my fingers. He kept his cold hands upon mine, following them as they sped along the ivory. The song felt somehow sadder to me now than I had ever realized. I don't think I had ever actually listened to the music as it pulsed through my fingers into the instrument. I was always too focused on playing the piece that I forgot to take the time to truly hear, and feel, the emotion behind it. I shut my eyes, allowing a warm drop of moisture to slip across my cheek as thoughts started welling inside my mind. It went unnoticed as Salem's eyes were focused on the movement of my hands.

Once the music faded, I collapsed into his arms. He didn't understand why I had begun bawling, and I didn't take the chance to explain it to him. He simply held me, which was all I wanted, all I needed at that moment. The realization of all that had happened within the last few months came back to me through the song all at once – losing my mother – twice – gaining a father, dropping out of school, nearly dying, falling in love ... I wiped my eyes and looked into his piercing blue stare, which darted back and forth from my face to the piano.

"I had never noticed how beautiful it is," I said between what was a mixture of a sob and a laugh.

Salem merely smiled and held my face in both hands, "Nor had I," he said, but he wasn't talking about the music as he stared longingly at my face. He kissed me tenderly once more, and then pulled away. "What do you call that tune, anyway?"

I thought for a moment, and then my lips curved into a simple smile. "*Nevermore.*"

The End

Thank you very much for reading Twin Souls!

I know your time is valuable, and I sincerely thank you for finishing my novel. If you would take a brief moment to return to an online book retailer and leave a review it would be much appreciated!

Reviews help new readers find my work and accurately decide if the book is for them as well as provide valuable feedback for my future writing.

Also, if you enjoyed the book, please be sure to tell a friend and check out the rest of the books in the Nevermore series!

Thank you again, and be sure to sign up to my mailing list to be alerted of new releases, giveaways, and more! http://www.kaylapoe.com/mailing-list

About the Author

KA Poe lives in Arizona with her husband and daughter. Someday she hopes to travel the world and live life to the fullest she possibly can. Writing has always been her passion. When she isn't writing she spends a lot of time reading, playing computer games, browsing the web, and spending time with her family. She has a vivid imagination, an eccentric personality and collects colorful socks.

To learn more about the author please visit her website at:
http://www.kaylapoe.com

Find her on Facebook at:
http://www.facebook.com/kaylapoe

Follow her on Twitter at:
http://www.twitter.com/KAPoeAuthor

Or e-mail her at:
kayla.a.poe@gmail.com

Also please sign up for the newsletter to be notified of new releases!
http://www.kaylapoe.com/mailing-list

Also By

Be sure to check these other novels by K.A. Poe!

THE NEVERMORE SERIES
Twin Souls
Hybrid
Sacrifice
Destiny

THE FOREVERMORE SERIES
Kismet
Catalyst

THE ANI'MARI SAGA
Ephemeral
Evanescent

THE AVARIAL TRILOGY
The King's Hourglass
The Phantom's Gift

DARIUS (Serial)
Through the Rift

Printed in Great Britain
by Amazon.co.uk, Ltd.,
Marston Gate.